Out of the Darkness

DEBRAH GISH

Out of the Darkness
Copyright © 2024 by Debrah Gish

ISBN: 979-8991517935 (sc)
ISBN: 979-8991517942 (e)

All rights reserved. No part of this publication may be reproduced, distributed, or transmitted in any form or by any means, including photocopying, recording, or other electronic or mechanical methods, without the prior written permission of the publisher and/or the author, except in the case of brief quotations embodied in critical reviews and other noncommercial uses permitted by copyright law.

The views expressed in this book are solely those of the author and do not necessarily reflect the views of the publisher, and the publisher hereby disclaims any responsibility for them.

Riverview Press

info@riverview-press.com
www.riverview-press.com

This book, Out of the Darkness, is lovingly dedicated to my daughter-in-love, Gina. She is forever filling the gap and she's a blessing to our family.

Contents

Chapter 1 1
Chapter 2 4
Chapter 3 10
Chapter 4 15
Chapter 5 21
Chapter 6 28
Chapter 7 34
Chapter 8 44
Chapter 9 50
Chapter 10 58
Chapter 11 63
Chapter 12 76
Chapter 13 84
Chapter 14 94
Chapter 15 109
Chapter 16 120
Chapter 17 130
Chapter 18 140
Chapter 19 153
Chapter 20 164
Chapter 21 170
Chapter 22 179
Epilogue 187

Chapter 1

Callie Hinson locked the door of her beauty salon and walked around the corner to her car. Thankful for the street and security lights of the other businesses, she tossed her purse and work bag into the backseat. Before she left for home, she pulled into the parking lot of the local diner that was the best eating establishment in her small town. Hannah's Cafe had been a favorite hang out for young and old as long as Callie could remember. In her twenty-five years, she figured she had eaten as many meals at Hannah's as she had at her own home located two miles out of town.

"Hey, Callie," the cafe owner greeted her from behind the counter that was still full of customers sitting atop the red plastic covered stools.

"Hi, Hannah! How are you this evening?" Callie answered as she simultaneously greeted the locals that were randomly seated around the square tables in the small dining area.

"I'm doing fine, busy as always. I've got your favorite tonight. Meat loaf and all the trimmings. I baked Tom's favorite for dessert," she announced.

"Apple pie? He's going to appreciate that, Hannah. I'll take a whole pie and he can eat on it the rest of the week." Callie smiled and handed Hannah her money as she received the three styrofoam containers.

"How's Tom doing, Callie? We haven't seen him in town for several days," Hannah mentioned.

"He's doing fine. The farm keeps him pretty busy, but you know my dad," Callie laughed. "He would not be happy if he wasn't working on something." Callie waved her farewells and balanced her food as she went out the door.

The road leading out of town was deserted and Callie's bright lights lit the way to her childhood home. She passed several fields and wooded areas without a thought. About one-fourth of a mile from her driveway, a wooded area drew her attention. She slowed her car and looked into the woods at a distinct light that looked totally out of place. She watched the unwavering beacon until she reached her turn off.

Her house was mostly dark except for the kitchen area where she knew her dad would be waiting. For thirteen years now it had just been Callie and her dad. He had been both father and mother to her and they couldn't be closer. Even though it had been awkward at times, he had made sure she never missed out on events that were usually attended by mother and daughter. Of course, she had to admit, the ladies in their small town had always made themselves available to help Callie and include her, along with their own daughters. Her mother's close friends were especially thoughtful toward Callie. Even after thirteen years, Tessa Hinson was still missed by everyone that knew her.

"Hey, Dad," Callie called.

"Hi, Honey," Tom Hinson greeted as he rushed to help her unload her arms.

"Hannah sent your favorite dessert." Callie lifted the lids on their intended dinner.

"That apple pie of hers? Her pies could win a blue ribbon at any county fair," he declared.

"I'm pretty sure they have, Dad," Callie laughed.

They were still laughing as they sat across from each other at the kitchen table. Callie joined hands with her dad while he thanked God for the food and the blessings of the day. As usual, he also named friends and neighbors who needed special prayer.

While they ate, they talked over the events of the day with Callie doing most of the talking. Her dad had been on the farm the entire day while she had spent the day in town at her shop, so she had more stories to tell.

She again thought about the light in the woods just beyond their driveway. "Dad, is Mr. Browning or Mr. Givens camping with their Sunday school class again?"

"Not that I know of. Why?" He lifted his eyes from his plate.

"Well, I know they've taken their class camping in our woods just down the road before, so I wondered. When I was coming home from work tonight, I saw a light in the same woods. That's why I thought it might be the boys enjoying a camping trip before school starts back in a couple weeks," she explained.

"No, like I said, not that I know of. I'm sure they would've said something to me before they just set up camping in my woods."

"Yeah, I thought not. I wonder about that light," she trailed off in thought.

"I'll take a little trip to the woods in the morning and see if I can see any signs of an interloper," he declared as he cleaned up his pie.

"Now, Dad, why don't you call Sheriff Henry and let him check it out?" Callie suggested.

"No, he's a busy man. If I can't handle it, then I'll call him."

"Okay, but when you go, take your gun and be sure to take Wally. That dog would tackle a mountain lion for you," she stated.

"Yes," he laughed. "I believe he would."

Callie cleared the table of the disposable containers but she didn't miss her dad going from window to window as he looked through the darkness toward the woods.

Later as she lay in bed unwinding from her day, she couldn't dismiss the fact there was some unknown person camping in their woods. Who was it and what business did he have trespassing on private property without permission?

Chapter 2

The next morning as Callie drove to work, she slowed down and craned her neck as she passed the woods. She saw nothing.

She went about her work, talking and joking with her customers, but the thought of her dad confronting some unknown person or persons in their woods troubled her.

After work, Callie closed her shop and hurried to the diner to pick up their usual dinner. She was friendly as always to Hannah and the customers having their evening meal but she didn't tarry. She was anxious to get home and hear what her dad had to tell her.

It was already dark again as she drove past the woods. She didn't have to look long at all until she spotted the bright light in the same spot as last night. She parked her car in the driveway beside her dad's pick up and scooped up her food and hurried inside. For some reason, she didn't feel safe with some unknown person able to see her and she couldn't see him... or her...or them. Callie had no idea if there was one person in their woods or a dozen. She hoped her dad could give some answers to her questions.

Callie and her dad set out the food containers and she started her inquiry.

"Okay, Dad, did you see the person in our woods?"

"Oh, yeah, I saw him," he answered calmly.

"So, it's a man?" Callie asked. "Only one?"

"Yeah, just one," he confirmed.

"And, you talked to him?"

"Yep, I talked to him."

"Well, who is he, dad? What's his name?" she questioned.

"He told me his name is Marc."

"Marc? Marc who?" She probed deeper. "What's his last name?"

"I don't know. He didn't say," he answered, still calm as could be.

"What do you mean, he didn't say? Didn't you ask him?" Her voice rose in exasperation.

"No. He's a grown man and I'm a grown man. He doesn't have to tell me anything."

"But, Dad!" she protested. "He's an interloper on your land!"

"Oh, he's not hurting anything. I'm not doing anything with that woods right now."

"Well, where's he from?"

"I don't know. He didn't tell me," he repeated.

"And you didn't ask, did you?" she reprimanded him.

"Nope. I didn't ask."

"What is he doing here in our little corner of the world?" she spouted.

"He didn't say," he calmly kept on eating.

Callie knew her dad was trying to end the conversation and eat his dinner but she wasn't satisfied at all with his answers to her questions. Or non-answers would be more like it.

"But, Dad, we don't know anything about this stranger. He could be a fugitive from justice or worse yet, he could be a serial killer." She laid out her fears for him to see.

"Now, Honey, stop worrying so. I don't think he means any harm to anyone."

"Well, Dad, you may not feel so charitable to him if he burns your woods down. The fire could cross the field and get all the way to the house," she informed him.

"Oh, his fire won't get away from him. He has one of those fire pits."

"A fire pit!" she exclaimed. "How did he get a fire pit all the way back there? What is he using for transportation? His feet? A bicycle? A motorcycle?" Callie rushed her questions.

"Oh, Callie," he laughed. "He's not using any of those modes of transportation. He has a car, an SUV to be exact. A real nice vehicle, I might add."

"How in the world did he get a vehicle back in the woods? There's trees everywhere!" she wondered out loud.

"By real good driving, I'd say," he joked.

"Oh, Dad, I don't like this. I wish you'd get more serious about this," she lamented.

"Now, Callie-girl, don't fret so," he tried to comfort her.

"Well, Dad, I know I can't tell you what to do about the stranger but if he steals you blind, or worse, don't say I didn't warn you!" she blurted out.

"Fair enough," he commented and calmly continued eating his pie.

Callie was too anxious to eat. She finally closed the top on her food container and decided she would eat it the next day for lunch. She couldn't believe how relaxed her dad was when only a field away, there was a man with no name and no past. Why wasn't he as curious as she? Maybe the man would be gone the next day. She could only hope.

With her housework caught up, Callie joined her dad in the living room. He was calmly reading the newspaper while she anxiously walked from window to window, looking in the direction of the light shining in the woods.

Later, lying in bed, Callie thought of the danger she and her dad were potentially in. She didn't understand her dad's reluctance to be suspicious of the stranger. Maybe her dad was losing some of his reasoning. She had to admit to herself that he still seemed mentally sharp. He could calculate and accomplish hard jobs just as good as he ever could.

Well, she determined, her dad might be gullible where the interloper was concerned but she was going to have her eyes on him and her ear to the ground. If he was a wanted man or had it in his mind to do mischief, she should hear about it in her beauty salon or the local diner. It seemed that every rumor in their small town was run through those two places before it made its way to the rest of the town's residents.

She was going to be on his trail for sure, and if he made one wrong move, she was calling the sheriff, with or without her dad's approval.

The next morning the tell tale signs of a restless night were evident on her face. The dark circles under her eyes could be covered up with concealing cream but she couldn't do anything about the frequent yawns that crept upon her.

Callie's day ended a little earlier than usual due to a last minute cancellation. Since she was getting home before dark, she decided to cook dinner instead of getting it from the diner. She enjoyed cooking but time-wise, she ordered their dinner most nights.

She found her dad in the yard, fastening a container on the back of his four wheeler.

"What's in your container, Dad? Weed killer?"

"Just water."

"Oh. What are you hauling water for? What are you going to do with it?"

He paused and finished securing the water can on the back of his ATV. "I'm taking it to Marc. He's almost out of water. He offered to walk up here and carry water back to his camp but that's too far to walk and carry water."

"So, you saw him again today?" she inquired.

"Yeah. I thought I'd just check on him and see if he needed anything."

Callie sighed in frustration. "Dad, you know this is dangerous. You don't know him. He could attack and rob you. Don't you realize that?"

"Now, Callie, he's not that way," he assured her. "Besides, I have Wally with me."

Callie thought a minute. "How does Wally react to the stranger?"

"Oh, he just smells of him and goes off wagging his tail," he chuckled. "The man is not a threat, Callie."

"Dad, you don't know that! You know nothing about him," she fretted.

"Callie, he's tried to pay me for the use of those woods. Now if he was planning to rob me, why would he try to give me money?" he reasoned.

"Well, I don't know," she spouted. "But I still don't trust him."

"Daughter, you haven't laid eyes on him. You may change your mind once you meet him."

"Once I meet him? I have no plans whatsoever to meet him. I'm just counting the hours until he leaves our area," she insisted strongly.

"Well, suit yourself. As for me, I'm taking him this water." With that remark, he climbed on his ATV and rode away.

Callie watched him leave the yard and pull onto the road that went by the woods. He turned into the trees and she could no longer see him.

In a huff, she went into the house and to the kitchen to prepare dinner. She stood with the refrigerator door wide open and looked over the items inside. Feeling bad about the words exchanged between them, she decided to make one of her dad's favorite meals. She gathered the ingredients for a breakfast casserole and proceeded to mix the ingredients together.

While it baked in the oven, she changed out of her colorful uniform and set the table. She heard the ATV as it pulled back into the driveway. She was taking the golden brown dish from the oven just as her dad came through the door.

When he saw the dish on the table, his eyes lit up. "What did I do to deserve this?" he teased.

"Oh, just for being the best dad in the world," she teased back at him. Glad that the air was no longer strained between them, they sat down together for their dinner.

Callie talked about her day in the shop and the many customers that she cared for. Her dad listened and commented in all the right places, but they didn't talk about the subject that was on both of their minds.

Out of the Darkness

"Well, Callie, are you going to ask me about the stranger in the woods?" he finally asked.

"No, I guess not," she laughed. "You're old enough to know what you want to do. So, I give up."

"That's not like you to give up. When you were a little girl, you'd keep digging until you got to the bottom of the problem that had you perplexed. I doubt you've changed."

"You're right. Of course, I'm very curious about the stranger. I just hope you're not putting your trust in a bad person," she answered candidly.

"Well, it's not that I trust him, nor do I distrust him. It's just something about him. I really can't explain it." With those words he offered no further explanation.

"I'm just hoping he gets his nomad life out of his system soon and goes back to where he hails from. Then all will get back to normal."

Her dad just grinned at her long speech and continued to eat his dinner.

Callie cleared the table and loaded the dishwasher automatically but her mind was busy trying to come up with a plan to protect her dad from the stranger in the woods.

Chapter 3

Callie carried on her work business as usual but she could hardly wait to get home to check on her dad. She had no idea what to expect each day. One thing she did find out. Her dad paid a visit to Mr. Woodsman, as she called him, every day.

It had been a week since she had noticed the light in the woods. She had not caught even a glimpse of the stranger, nor did she want to. She knew her dad was keeping him supplied with fresh water and no telling what else. Was he taking him food? Was he giving him money? She had no idea and her dad was not telling.

On the ninth day, Callie came home from her work day to find her dad was no where to be found. She looked through the house and the barn. She called and called and finally heard him answer. She followed the voice which took her to the small barn directly behind the big one.

"Dad? Why didn't you answer me? I've called and called for you," she asked worriedly.

"Well, Daughter, for one thing, I didn't hear you. And another thing, I'm quite busy," he replied rather testily.

At his terse reply, Callie looked around her. One of her dad's favorite cows was on the ground and he was standing over her.

"Dad, what's wrong with Lizzie?" she wondered.

"She's trying to have her calf and she's having trouble," he explained.

"Do you want me to call Dr. James?" she asked.

"He's still in the hospital. Doc Miller is trying to cover for him but we don't have time to wait on him. Even if he wasn't out on a call, it would take him too long to get here. Lizzie is getting in real trouble," he declared.

"I can help, Dad. Just tell me what to do," she pushed up her sleeves.

"I appreciate it, Honey, but you just don't have the strength. Pure and simple."

"What can we do, Dad?" she worried.

"Nothing else we can do. I'm going to get Marc," he declared. "Stay with Lizzie."

Callie nodded silently and watched her dad jump on the four-wheeler and head towards the woods. Wally chased after his master but made a circle and came back to stand watch over the bawling cow. Within five minutes her dad was back and he was not alone. On the back of the ATV was the stranger. She was finally going to get a look at the mysterious Marc.

Her dad rushed back into the small barn with the younger man right on his heels. Both men ignored Callie but by this time, she felt so sympathetic for the hurting cow that she didn't pay much attention to them either.

Callie watched her dad as he gave orders and the stranger obeyed each one. Just when she thought Lizzie and her baby would be lost, two little hoofs appeared, then legs and finally a small replica of its mother lay on the hay with its sides heaving.

The two men let out a cry of satisfaction at the same time. Callie was quiet but the grin on her face showed her feelings.

"Marc, you acted just like an old farm hand! Are you sure you haven't done this before?" Tom Hinson exclaimed.

"No, Sir!" The stranger laughed, "I promise this is the first time."

Callie's attention was diverted from the calf to the man kneeling in the hay beside the cow. His voice was strong and refined. His laugh was pleasant. *Who is this man,* Callie thought, *and what drove him to take up residence all alone in our woods?* She had many questions but no answers. The only thing she knew was, for some reason, her father liked this man.

"Let's go wash up at the water hose, then we'll go inside and get a proper wash," her dad directed.

They headed toward the rolled up water hose and Callie bypassed them and went into the house to do her own washing and tend to the dinner that had been slowly cooking since morning. She put rolls in the oven and prepared the lettuce and salad makings. Did she set the table for two or three? Her dad would let her know. After the events in the barn, she figured the stranger would be offered a hot meal. Would he accept or retreat back into the woods?

The outside door opened and her dad ushered the stranger inside as he would an old friend.

"Callie, set Marc a place at our table. After all that work, I'm sure he's hungry," he said, as he passed through on the way to wash up properly.

"Oh, no Sir. That's not necessary. I'll just wash and go back to the camp," he insisted.

"I'll not hear of it! You're going to eat with us. That's the least we can do," Tom Hinson stated.

Callie nodded quietly at her father and the stranger looked uncomfortable. For some reason that brought her pleasure.

While the men washed up in the hall bathroom, Callie set the table for three. When they returned, the food, along with their plates, was on the table.

The stranger sat at the table quietly, waiting for his host to take the lead. Tom Hinson stuck out his hands to his two table mates. Callie held tightly to her father's hand but couldn't bring herself to reach for the hand of Marc whoever. While her father prayed, she fought the urge to take a peek at the stranger.

The men dug into the food before them and Callie couldn't help but observe the stranger as he ate. His manners were impeccable from the way he held his fork, to the way he cut his chicken with his knife. He was more of a mystery than ever. What kind of man lives in the woods like the homeless, but holds his knife and fork like a man at a fancy banquet?

As they ate, her dad made normal conversation and the stranger answered when he was required, using only one or two words. Callie ate in silence. She didn't want to appear mad or hostile but she figured she owed this stranger nothing.

Sure, he had helped her dad and had probably saved the life of Lizzie and her baby, but for nine days, he had been living in their woods free of charge. So, in her mind, they were even.

While he ate, Callie got a chance to really observe him. He was neat in appearance, dressed in jeans and a pullover shirt, and a pair of expensive gym shoes. His black hair was in need of a trim but still passable. He had a full short beard that she figured he'd only been growing since he had been vagabonding. He was on the handsome side of the scale but the mystery that surrounded him erased all else.

He cleaned his plate before she was half finished and she was a little surprised when he stood and took his dishes to the sink. "Thank you both for a delicious meal. I'll be getting back to the camp now. Goodnight," he added.

"Wait! Wait, Marc! I'll take you back on the four wheeler," Tom Hinson stood up.

"No, that's not necessary, Mr. Hinson. The moon is bright and I can see all right. I'll enjoy the walk," the stranger insisted.

"Well, I sure thank you for helping with Lizzie." Tom Hinson stuck out his hand. The stranger looked at the extended hand and finished the handshake.

"I'm glad I could help," he answered, nodded his goodnight to Callie, and went out the door.

Callie played with her food while her mind was on the silent man walking down their driveway. Finally, her silence had reached its limit. "Dad, who is that guy?" she asked in exasperation.

"His name is Marc," he answered with his eyes twinkling.

Their eyes met and they both broke out laughing. That told Callie that her dad knew no more about the stranger than he had the week before.

"Did you notice his clothes, Dad? They're definitely not bargain basement clothes. He's been camping in the woods for nine days but he's as clean as a pin. His fingernails were clean and trimmed and he used his knife and fork as if he was at a formal banquet. Did you notice all that?"

"Yes, Daughter, I noticed all of that. There's a story that goes with that young man. I just don't know what it is," he admitted.

Callie sure didn't have any answers either.

Chapter 4

Since the stranger had helped save the cow, he had retreated back into the woods and Callie had not laid eyes on him for four days. She and her dad had not discussed the unknown man but she knew her dad had seen him daily. She didn't know how she knew, but she just knew.

He had been living in the woods for thirteen days when her dad casually mentioned the stranger.

"Callie, I let Marc wash his clothes here today. He asked about a place in town to do his laundry but I insisted he could use ours."

"Dad! You didn't!" Callie raised her voice.

"Of course, I did," he replied calmly.

"But, Dad!"

"Callie, Honey, the man doesn't have leprosy," he teased.

"Dad, we don't know one thing about him," she reasoned. "There's no telling how he left my clean washer and dryer!" She took off toward the small laundry room. What she saw stopped her in her tracks. The washer was gleaming clean and so was the dryer. There was not a speck of grass or trash to be seen. Even the lint filter had been cleaned. The clean state of her laundry appliances only proved to deepen the mystery about the man camping in their woods.

On Saturdays, Callie worked only half days, so her Saturday afternoons were usually taken up with housework, laundry and preparing for Sunday dinner.

Sundays were just about the only day that her dad left the farm. Sunday mornings were spent in church and then they enjoyed whatever Callie had prepared for their lunch.

Tom Hinson pushed himself back from the table.

"Callie, you out did yourself today. That meatloaf is superb. Those little garlic potatoes are delicious. Where did you learn to cook them that way?"

"One of my customers brought me that recipe. I think it's a keeper," she smiled.

"Callie, I wish you'd fix a nice big plate of this food and I'll run it down to our neighbor," he suggested.

"Dad!"

"Callie!" He barked right back. "The man is right down the road and we barely made a dent in this meal."

"But, Dad!" she argued.

"Callie, this is Sunday. The Lord's Day. Why don't we act like it? Now, I agree, Marc is carrying a heavy load. How, what, or why? I have no idea, but we need to act like Christians and be a help to him if we can. What would your mama do?"

"Oh, Dad, that's not fair and you know it. You know what mom would do. She would cook him three hot meals a day and snacks in between," she couldn't hold back a laugh.

"Exactly!" He commented.

"Okay, you win. I'll fix it," she conceded. She loaded a plate as full as she could get it without it running over the sides. She found a small box in the laundry room that was just the right size to pack the plate, a wedge of chocolate cake, and a large glass of tea, along with eating utensils wrapped in a bundle of table napkins.

"Here you go, Dad," Callie pushed the box toward him.

"Thank you, Honey." He looked into the box. "I know he's going to enjoy this. You're more like your mama than you think." He picked up the box, balanced it on his four-wheeler and took off for the woods.

She watched her dad travel slower than usual to keep from losing the box chocked full of Sunday dinner. One thing for certain, Mr. Woodsman had a secret of some sort. Her dad could probably weasel his secret out of him but it was doubtful she would ever hear it. That's the kind of man her father is, loyal and trusting to a fault.

On Mondays, Callie always closed her shop. She spent time in her mother's flower beds, cleaning out every weed that dared to grow there. Callie remembered clearly how her mother had loved her flowers and letting them be taken over by weeds was not an option.

When the flower beds were finished, Callie showered and then fired up the grill. While the pork chops grilled, Callie prepared vegetables. The gallon of tea setting in the sun was her dad's favorite and the vegetables were from their own garden.

She timed the cooking of the food to coincide with the time that her dad would finish his work day. Callie grilled a couple more pork chops and cooked extra vegetables just in case her dad felt he needed to feed the loner in the woods. She smiled at the way her dad insisted on helping the man that they knew nothing about. Not even his name. It wasn't like her dad to take in strangers, yet, it was like him to lend a helping hand to anyone that needed it.

The stranger had been in the woods for more than two weeks and, as far as she could tell, nothing had gone missing at the farm and the two banks in town hadn't been robbed. She had to laugh at her own thoughts. She had a suspicion that one morning they would wake up and the woods dweller would be gone and never heard from again.

The end of August meant that the summer would be ending and fall would be taking its place, along with the cooler temperatures. With that thought in mind, Callie set the picnic table for their evening meal. The food came off the grill about the same time her dad came back from his washing.

"Oh, Callie-girl, this meal looks wonderful," he commented.

"I thought we'd eat outside while we still can. The cold wind will start soon. And the garden is about finished. I'm going to miss these fresh vegetables," she mentioned.

When they finished their meal, he eyed the pork chops and the vegetables still on the table.

"Callie, do you think we could spare some of this food for Marc?"

"Yes, Dad," she laughed. "I thought you'd want to divide with our neighbor, as you call him. I'll fix him a plate." She proceeded to do just that but certainly didn't expect her dad's next question.

"Do you want to ride with me? I'll get your ATV out of the shed," he offered.

"Not on your life!" she blurted out with her eyes snapping.

"Well, I just thought...I think he needs a friend, Honey."

"Well, it's not going to be me!" She glared at the plate she was loading up.

"Oh, I didn't mean anything like that," he apologized. "I just think he wants to belong somewhere but he doesn't know where. That's all."

"He'll find his niche one day. I figure it will be far away from here," she hoped.

Her dad took the plate filled with grilled food and a quart jar of ice cold tea. Callie watched him and determined that he was getting quite good at balancing a box of food with one hand and steering the four-wheeler with the other. She sent up a silent prayer that the stranger would not take advantage of her generous dad. Or worse.

The next day, Callie's work day was long and didn't end until way past dark. She stopped at the diner and picked up her called in order. Hannah didn't comment on the extra food that was ordered and Callie didn't offer up a reason.

At home, Callie unloaded the food from the white diner bag.

"Here, Dad. This is yours, this one is mine, and this one is for your nameless stray," she laughed.

"Oh, he has a name."

"Of course, he does! Marc!" They laughed as they simultaneously said his first name.

He took the food and headed for the woods with the headlights leading the way with the family dog trailing safely behind. Callie just shook her head at her dad's actions toward the trespasser in the woods.

Every Thursday was walk-in day at Callie's shop. Some Thursdays Callie was kept busy and some others could be slow. On this Thursday, the morning was extra busy with kids haircuts in anticipation of school starting in just a few days. Callie ate her customary lunch sandwich then got busy with more arriving customers. Mid-afternoon, there was a lull in customers and Callie took advantage of the free time to do a little housekeeping. She ran the vacuum in her shop and was just putting it away when the chime over the door drew her back into the shop. She stopped in mid-step when she saw her next customer.

"Uh...Miss Hinson, your dad said you give men haircuts, also?" he questioned.

"Yes, of course, I do," she finally managed to answer. "Do you want a haircut?"

"Yes, Ma'am, I do. Uh...I went to the barber shop down the street but it was closed. So I thought I'd try here..." he trailed off.

"I know. The barber, Mr. Frank, is on vacation. He and his wife are in Illinois waiting for their first grandchild to be born."

"Could you, by any chance, give me a trim?" he asked.

"I certainly can. Have a seat." She pointed to her empty chair and covered him with a fresh cape. "Okay, how do you want it cut?"

"Just give me a good trim. I haven't had a haircut in weeks," he replied.

Callie picked up her scissors and began cutting. She was surprised how soft and clean his hair was which didn't make sense for a man camping in the woods. For a vagabond, it seems he was really careful about his hygiene.

Callie tried to think of something to say but couldn't even find a subject to make small talk about. She suspected he was having the same problem, but maybe not. After all, he was spending all of his time in the woods alone. That was another puzzling fact. If he didn't want to see anyone, why would he be so careful about his personal care? And why would he care about the length of his hair?

When she finished his haircut, she spun his chair around to face the mirror.

"Does this look okay? If not, tell me what to change," she suggested.

"Oh, it's fine. It looks nice. Thank you."

She brushed his neck one final time and removed his cape and he stood. He reached for his wallet and laid two bills on the counter.

"Oh,no, Mr....Sir. The haircut is only one of these bills. She took one and handed the other one back to him.

"No. You keep it, Miss Hinson. Consider it a down payment on some of that good food I've been enjoying," he grinned slightly and went out the door.

Callie stared at the money still in her hand. He was more of a mystery than ever. She wondered what his story was. Like her dad, she was beginning to think he was no threat to anyone except himself. Whatever was behind his solitary living, he needed to talk it out with someone. One thing she was glad about, that someone would not be her.

Chapter 5

That night while Callie and her dad were having dinner, she told him about her surprise customer.

"Dad, guess who came into the shop this afternoon?"

"Uh...Marc, maybe?"

"How did you know?" She asked sternly. "Did you send him to me for a haircut?"

"Nope. But yesterday, he asked where he could get a haircut. I sent him to Frank's," he countered.

"He did say he went there first but the barber shop was closed," she recalled. "Mr. Frank and his wife are in Illinois waiting for the arrival of their first grandchild."

"Oh, I didn't know that."

"So, I gave him a haircut," she declared. "Dad, I don't get it. He has been living in the woods for nearly three weeks, but it's strange. He was as clean as could be. He didn't even smell like wood smoke. I remember when Dirk and I were younger, you and mom would take us camping. We had a blast but we couldn't wait to get home and wash off the camping crud and the smell of wood smoke. What's going on with this guy?"

"Well, I do know he showers everyday. He's got himself a shower rigged up back there," he chuckled. "He's got every new fangled gadget imaginable."

"I wonder what he's going to do when the weather gets cooler," Callie pondered out loud.

Her dad shrugged his shoulders, "I have no idea. Did he talk to you at all while you were cutting his hair?"

"Well no but, I couldn't think of a single thing to say to him either," she admitted. "Does he talk to you?"

"Oh, yes, we talk a lot, but about the weather and his camping gadgets mostly," he laughed. "But nothing about his last name, where he's from, or why he's living like a hermit."

"Dad, I brought him a meal from Hannah's, if you want to take it to him." She slid the styrofoam container across the table.

"Yeah, I will. I don't want him to be hungry."

"Oh, I doubt that he's going hungry. If he's as well-equipped as you say, I'm sure he has enough trail mix to tide him over," she laughed. "But, he can't live on snacks, so take him some food."

Tom Hinson took off for the woods immediately on the ATV, using the headlights to see. Callie knew he wouldn't be back for a while, so she tossed away the disposable dinner cartons and looked through the stack of mail on the counter. She threw away the junk mail and put the utility bills in the crystal fruit bowl to be paid.

Over an hour later, her dad pulled into the yard and entered the house.

"I was beginning to think that you were spending the night in the woods, too," she teased.

"I tell you, Honey," he laughed, "I don't think I could survive a night in the woods anymore. I don't think my old bones could take it. Marc sleeps in a hammock. He says he sleeps like a baby. I'm not sure I believe him," he chuckled.

"Did he eat the food?"

"Of course. He never turns down food but he tries to pay me every time," he answered.

"Today after his haircut, he paid me double. I tried my best to give the extra money back to him but he wouldn't take it. He said to consider it a down payment on food he's been eating. I wonder where he gets his money," she paused. "Do you think he's a bank robber?"

Her dad burst out laughing and she had to join him. She didn't know anything about the man, but, for some unknown reason, she didn't think he'd gotten his money dishonestly.

Before she went to bed, she stood at the window and watched the light in the woods. Marc showing up in their woods was still a mystery. Where did he come from, and why was he keeping to himself? It was apparent that something was troubling him, but would he ever have the courage or inclination to seek help?

With a long sigh, she turned from the window. She couldn't help him and was pretty sure she didn't want to get too involved in his troubles. So she would keep her distance and pray for him and if her prayers were answered, he'd go back to his former life and the light would be gone from the woods.

****

When Callie returned home on Saturday, after her half day of work, she was met in the driveway by her dad.

"Hey, Daughter! How was work this morning?"

"Work was just fine, thank you. I had five haircuts, four shampoos, and that's all," she laughed.

"Well, I hope you're not too tired because we have an invitation to dinner," he informed her.

"Oh, really? Where are we going?" she asked as she gathered her purse and work bag from her car.

"Uh….we're going to the woods. Marc invited us to eat dinner with him," he blurted out.

Callie wheeled to face her dad. "No, Dad, I'm not going. You can go if you want, but I have no desire to go eat with someone who won't share as much as his last name."

"Oh, Honey, don't be that way. If he is around us more, maybe he'll open up a bit more about himself," he reasoned.

"Nope. Let him open up to you. I don't want to know anything about the man. The only thing I want to know is when is he going to vacate our woods and go away," she exclaimed.

"Why, Callie, that's not like you. You always took in every stray cat or dog that came around. Just like your mama," he reminded her.

"Dad, this is not a stray dog or cat. This is a man that we know nothing about and he wants nothing to do with anyone. So, I'm just giving him what he wants. Solitude," she ended her tirade.

Her dad just stood and looked at her. He nodded and walked away. The slump of his shoulders told her how disappointed he was. Well, she couldn't help his hurt feelings. There were some things she just was not prepared to do and one of those things was eat dinner in a mosquito infested woods with a stranger.

Callie went into the house and out of frustration, she threw herself into her housework. Most Saturdays, she accomplished her housework at her leisure but not today. She worked non-stop and two hours later she put away the vacuum and her cleaning supplies.

She looked in the refrigerator to decide what to cook for dinner. Since her dad would not be joining her for the evening meal, she decided on an omelet for herself.

Her dad came into the house, showered, put on clean jeans and a plaid shirt. He was quiet, which was unusual for him. Callie couldn't stand to disappoint him. She struggled within herself, but finally gave in. "Dad, if you'll give me twenty minutes to get ready, I'll go with you," she conceded.

His eyes lit up and a smile appeared on his face. "Sure, Honey. Take all the time you need. I'll wait!"

Callie showered in record time and dressed quickly. As she stood looking into the mirror, she debated on how much makeup to wear and what to do with her hair. She applied a tinted moisture and a touch of mascara and considered it enough for a trek to the woods. Her shoulder

Out of the Darkness

length blond hair could be styled many ways, but, for the woods, she decided on a ponytail. She took one last look in the mirror, and couldn't believe what she was about to do.

At four o'clock, Callie and her dad climbed on their ATV's and headed for the woods, with Tom Hinson taking the lead. They pulled into the wooded camping area to be met by their host.

"Welcome! I'm glad you both could make it," he greeted them.

Callie looked around the camping area, missing nothing. His black, expensive SUV was parked on one side and his tent was set up on the opposite side. In the middle was a clearing that had a fire pit, a grill, and a card table with three canvas camping chairs. A large cooler was close to the grill. There was a knitted hammock strung between two trees. The back door of his vehicle was up and she could see a plastic pan that held laundry supplies. A clothing bar, filled with clothes, reached from one side to the other. Shoes and boots were lined up neatly on one side in the back. Once, when he opened the driver's side door, Callie got a glimpse of a laptop computer and a stack of books.

She made herself focus on the conversation going on around her. Their host kept up a conversation with her dad, even as he lifted three beautiful steaks from the ice filled cooler. Next, he cut three large baking potatoes, seasoned and buttered them before wrapping them in foil and arranging on the grill. Other vegetables were cut and seasoned to be cooked beside the potatoes.

"May I help?" Callie offered.

"No, thank you, Miss Hinson. It's my turn to feed you and Mr. Hinson instead of the other way around," he refused quietly.

Callie left him to his work and explored more of his campsite. On the other side of his vehicle was some kind of contraption that she was having trouble identifying. There was a round cylinder covered with heavy plastic. Above the cylinder was a huge plastic bucket. She thought and thought, until it finally dawned on her that it must be his shower. She bit back a laugh at the sight of his lopsided home rigged shower.

She sauntered back to the cooking area and watched the man doing the cooking. The way he turned the steaks and arranged the vegetables, told her he was not a novice at cooking. She wanted to help but he had refused her once and she didn't want a repeat.

When the steaks were cooked, Marc laid one on each disposable plate and then added the potatoes and the grilled vegetables.

Callie hadn't eaten since breakfast and she had to admit, the food looked delicious. The aroma from the sizzling steaks tantalized her taste buds and made her stomach feel emptier than ever. When he announced the food was ready, she didn't hesitate.

They occupied the three chairs around the square table and Marc looked at her dad.

"I believe you pray before meals, Mr. Hinson," he stated.

"Do you mind?" Tom Hinson asked.

"No. No, of course not," he assured him.

This time Callie couldn't refuse to take the hand that reached out to her. After all, she was sitting at his table, eating his food, and he was sitting less than a foot from her. She couldn't help but notice his hands were not covered with calluses but they weren't soft either. What kind of work did this man do before he turned up here? Probably not construction or any hard labor, she determined. But what?

Tom Hinson prayed and Callie missed it all except the amen. She felt guilty for letting her mind wander while something as important as praying was happening. If her suspicion was correct, Marc whoever could use some prayers.

Even though Callie hadn't wanted to make the trip to eat at the campsite, she was glad she had come if not for the food alone. She didn't remember eating a steak that tasted as good. It was cooked to perfection and she wondered how he got it so tender. The vegetables were absolutely delicious. She felt she needed to tell him so "Uh...Marc, Uh...Sir," she stammered, "this meal is wonderful. My compliments to the chef."

"Thank you, Miss Hinson. The chef accepts your compliments," he laughed.

"Do you cook very much?" she ventured to ask.

"At times," he answered.

Callie knew he wasn't going to tell her anything else so she quit pushing. She finished her meal in silence and listened to the men carry on a friendly conversation. They talked about the different trees that surrounded them, as well as the starting winter. Her dad talked of the fall harvesting that would be coming in just a few days.

When they finished eating, Marc started a fire in the fire pit and covered it with a steel rack, then added an old fashioned coffee pot. Callie usually drank coffee only at breakfast but the boiling coffee smelled amazing. When the coffee was finished, their host poured the dark liquid into three glass mugs. Cream and sugar was passed around but Callie was the only taker. This was the first time in her twenty-five years that she'd had coffee made in such a manner. She had to admit it was quite enjoyable.

They sat around the fire pit for the better part of an hour. The silence was interrupted occasionally by small talk but mostly they just sat and looked into the fire. Her early morning schedule, along with the soothing of the fire began to work on Callie. She changed her position to shake off the sleepiness.

"I believe I'll go on home, Dad. I'll probably be in bed when you get home," she directed at her dad. She then turned to their host.

"Thank you, Sir, for a wonderful meal. It was quite enjoyable," she said awkwardly.

"You're quite welcome, Miss Hinson. Thank you for coming," he answered. "But you shouldn't go back alone. You need to wait for your dad."

Her dad stood, "I agree, Marc. It's time I went, too. My bedtime is getting closer," he laughed.

With one last goodnight, Callie and her dad climbed back on their four-wheelers and drove home.

Chapter 6

The next day at church, Callie thought about their mysterious neighbor. She was more convinced than ever that he was hiding something, or maybe he was just extremely troubled. Whatever was going on with him, he needed help. She whispered a prayer for the man that didn't have a last name, or one that he would share anyway.

For lunch, Callie and her dad enjoyed BLT sandwiches, using their own garden tomatoes and lettuce. Callie fried extra bacon just in case her dad wanted to share with his friend.

"Dad, do you want to take your friend a sandwich?" she asked.

"Sure, if you'll fix it up," he agreed.

Callie made two large sandwiches loaded with crispy bacon and vegetables. She wrapped them and added a thermos of sweet tea. Just as her dad was going out the door with the small box under his arm, Callie stopped him.

"Dad, tell your friend that he can use my ATV, if he wants. I hardly ever ride it and he may want to ride around the farm when you start taking in the crops."

"Really? Does that mean you are beginning to trust him?" he asked candidly.

"No," she answered, "but I trust you. You've never been wrong about a person yet."

He paused at her statement. "Well, I'll be back after while." He went out the door without another word.

Callie always enjoyed her Mondays. Her day was spent mostly the same each week. She'd do housework, a little cooking and try to spend some quality time in the yard swing under the large oak trees. With a small stack of unread magazines, she headed for the swing. With Wally curled comfortably at her feet, she lost track of time. Nearly an hour had passed while she was engrossed in an article, she didn't know anyone was around until he spoke.

"Miss Hinson?"

Callie jumped and turned to face her nameless neighbor. "Oh, uh, yes?" she finally managed to say.

"Your father said you offered me the use of your ATV. That's very generous of you and I wanted to personally thank you," he declared.

"You're welcome. I don't ride it much anymore. Next week, my dad will be gathering in his crops, so he'll be busy. You can ride the four-wheeler around the farm, if you like."

"I'll do just that," he stated. "I would be glad to help him if he needs me."

"Do you know anything about farming?" Callie asked.

"No. Not one thing," he laughed.

"I don't think that's true. You helped deliver Lizzie's baby a few weeks back," she reminded him.

"I don't think that counts," he refuted.

"Oh, I think Lizzie would beg to differ with you and so would my dad," she laughed. "By the way, are you curious about why we are so attached to Lizzie?"

"Well, yes. I have wondered. Especially why she gets special treatment when all the cows in the fields get no special attention."

"Lizzie is special. Her mama died when she was born and we raised Lizzie on a bottle. We even kept her in the house for several weeks until she got strong enough to be out in the barn. This was her first baby and dad says it will be her last. She's a little small to be having babies."

"Now I understand Mr. Hinson's panic that day. All they needed was a little more muscle. I'm glad I could provide it." He pointed to the other end of the swing opposite her. "May I?"

"Of course." Callie pulled the magazines closer to her.

"I'd like to talk to you, if you don't mind," he commented.

"All right," Callie paused, waiting for him to speak. She was a little perturbed when Wally stood, stretched himself and laid his head on the man's knee. The dog was rewarded with slow, gentle head scratches that made him close his eyes. *Traitor,* Callie silently accused him. When the man began talking, she had to focus on what he was saying.

"I want to thank you and your dad for allowing me to camp out on your property these last few weeks. I know you're both bound to be curious about me. Where I came from? Why I'm here?" He voiced her thoughts perfectly.

"Well," Callie laughed quietly. "We have been wondering about those facts."

"Yeah, I'm sure you have. It's complicated. I know where I'm from but I don't know why I'm here. What I'm doing on a farm in Michigan, I really can't say. I drove for days. I went to different cities, different states, even, but when I came to your little town, I was compelled to stop. I looked for a camping area because I had all of my equipment in my wagon. I ran up on your woods. It was just what I had been looking for. So...I stopped. I really intended to stay only one night then move on but here I am almost four weeks later," he finished.

"We've got a few more weeks until cooler weather. So, I guess, you're safe for the time being," she noted.

"Miss Hinson, I have a favor to ask of you. I've tried and tried to pay rent on the campsite but your dad won't let me. Would you talk to him and persuade him to take some rent from me?"

"Sorry, I can't do that. My dad makes the important decisions around here and I don't go against him."

Out of the Darkness

"But I want you and your father to know that I'm on the up and up. I'm not a bum. I just need a place to figure some things out."

"To be honest, Mr...Sir, we're not using the woods at the present time. So, there's no deadline you have to meet," Callie admitted.

"Thank you. I appreciate that. I don't know if you know it but your dad told me the same thing. I really like your dad, Miss Hinson. He is a good man."

"I couldn't agree more. He has been both father and mother to me since I was twelve years old. There's nothing I wouldn't do for him or do to protect him," she vowed.

"Is that a threat, Miss Hinson?" he asked.

"Not unless you mean him harm," she looked him in the eye. To her surprise, her comment drew a chuckle from him.

"I like that in a person. Love and loyalty are wonderful traits to have. I bet you would be the same way with your husband, wouldn't you?" he asked, pointedly.

"You better know it!" This time she was the one laughing.

"Tell me, Miss Hinson, would you have felt that way about Kent Phillips back in high school?" he asked with his eyes twinkling.

In shock, Callie turned to him. "Who told you about Kent?"

"Your dad, but don't be mad at him. I talked him into it," he admitted.

"And how did that conversation come about?" she demanded.

"Well, I asked him how was it that you, a full grown up, lovely, independent woman still lived at home?" he explained.

"Hmmm. Is that so?" she snapped at him.

"Since I've already put my foot in my mouth, what happened to you and this Kent fellow?"

"Not that it's any of your business, but I'll tell you. After our high school graduation, I went to school to be a hairdresser and Kent joined the military. When he came home on his leaves, we'd go out some. Also, we wrote letters back and forth occasionally. When he was discharged, he

31

came home but didn't want to stay. He wanted a bigger town, so he left. He lives in Denver, Colorado now."

"Did you love him?" He didn't try to hide his curiosity.

"Oh, yes, I loved him, but I wasn't in love with him," she stressed.

"How do you know?"

"Because, when he left, I barely missed him. I didn't fall apart. As a matter of fact, I wished him well," she informed him.

"Did he ask you to go with him?" His question brought a laugh from her.

"He did say I could come, too."

"Were you tempted?"

"Not in the least," she answered testily.

"Why not?"

"Why are you so nosey?" she asked. "I don't expect you to understand but I love this little town and the people in it. This town helped my dad raise me after my mom died. This is my home," she said finally.

He sat quietly as though mulling over her words. "That's a very powerful reason. Home. That word has a wonderful sound," he said quietly.

"You have a home, too. Some place where you are loved. A place where you are probably missed," she assured him.

"I am from somewhere, of course. But it's not home like it is here."

"Well, it could be," she pointed out. "What about your family? A wife, maybe? Or a fiance? Your parents? Siblings?"

"No wife. No siblings. Parents, yes," he admitted.

"Well, that's something," she stressed. "Now, where is home?" She watched the curtain come down and he clammed up. He stood and the swing raised as he lifted his weight.

"Maybe another time, Miss Hinson." He started toward the driveway, then stopped and turned. "Miss Hinson, my name is Marc Reed, but you can call me Marc."

Out of the Darkness

"Okay,...Marc," she complied.

"I know your name is Callie, but I won't call you that until you give me permission." He turned and walked toward the ATV waiting in the driveway with the dog trotting beside him.

Callie watched him drive to his refuge in the woods. The very idea, she fumed. Her dad telling the man about her past anything, aggravated her. The more she thought about it, she began to see the humor in the whole situation. The man, Marc, had a way of making someone talk. After all, she had spilled the whole story of herself and Kent. No harm done, she decided. She had nothing to be ashamed of or to hide. But she couldn't say the same about the man camping in their woods.

Chapter 7

Since the loan of Callie's ATV, Marc Reed had been around much more. It wasn't strange at all for her to look out the window and see him at the barn with her dad. One thing for sure, her dad had definitely found a friend. When the man decided to move on, her dad would miss him.

Callie hadn't had much interaction with Marc Reed since their talk a few days earlier. Most nights Callie had sent her dad to the woods with dinner for their neighbor, and he had repaid them by helping her dad around the farm. She had to laugh when her dad told her about giving Marc driving lessons on the tractor. Her laugh didn't last long because she found out he was a good student and a fast learner, according to her dad.

She had to reluctantly admit she was glad Marc was there with her dad, as she left for work each morning. Along with two hired men helping Marc and her dad, the harvesting was ahead of schedule. Their farm was not as large as some in the area, but it was still plenty big, especially as her dad was getting older. Her dad had hired the same two men for years and with the addition of an extra man, things were going very well.

Callie had been the bookkeeper for her dad since high school. At the end of the first week, he brought her a sheet of paper with the hours worked by the two hired men and Marc. She totaled up the hours for each man and filled out their checks accordingly.

"Dad, when you take Marc's check, don't forget his dinner. It's on the counter," she reminded him.

"I won't forget. Callie, I want to thank you for sending his meals. He's been a real help to me."

"You're welcome, Dad. He's not a bad person," she laughed, "or at least, I don't think he is."

"No, he's the real deal. I'm sure of it. He's trying to work through some things. I don't know what his problem is but he's beginning to open up to both of us. He even told you his last name; that's something in itself."

"I know that but I looked on line for Marc Reed but none of the Marc Reeds that I found was our Marc Reed. He's still a mystery, Dad."

"Well, yes, in some ways, but in other ways, I feel like I know him pretty well," he countered.

"I'm sure he's hungry after working all day. I wonder what kind of work he did before he came here," she looked at her dad questioningly.

Tom Hinson shrugged his shoulders. "I have no idea, but right now he's a farmer." He laughed and went out the door with the checks in hand and a meal for their neighbor.

On Saturday afternoon, Callie hurried home from her half day at the shop and uncovered the gas grill. She had stopped at the supermarket for fresh items to be prepared to go with the burgers from their home freezer.

When the men left the barn, still talking, Callie walked out to meet them.

"Well, how's the harvesting coming?" she asked, pleasantly.

"Very well," her dad answered. "Having an extra man this year has been a big help." He turned his look on the younger man beside him.

"I'm glad I could help, Tom. Surprisingly, I'm enjoying it. I've never done anything like this before and I've learned so much."

"Well, Marc, I'm glad you've been here to help Dad. Now we want to do something for you. I'm going to throw some burgers and chicken on the grill, if you would like to join us."

"That sounds wonderful, I accept," he agreed. "I'll go to the camp and clean up first. May I go into town and get something to go with the meal?" He directed the question to Callie.

"We have everything. Just bring your appetite," she laughed.

"Now, that I can do," he teased back. "What time?" He looked at his watch.

"About three o'clock, maybe?" she answered.

"I'll be here." He walked to her four-wheeler and took off for his campsite, and of course, Wally was on his trail.

"Callie," her dad spoke beside her, "he refused the check you wrote last night. I insisted, but he wouldn't take it."

"But, Dad, he earned it. I wonder how he is living?"

"Now, that I don't know, but I don't think he is doing anything dishonest," he defended the near stranger.

"I hope not! I'd sure hate for Sheriff Henry to come out here and raid us," she remarked dryly.

"I don't think we have to worry about that," he commented, laughing. "Right now I'm going to get a shower, then I'll help you with that grilling."

While her dad was showering, Callie brought out the makings for their meal. The sound of her ATV coming down the driveway made her look at her watch. He was early. Oh well, he could visit with her dad while she grilled the meat and vegetables, she decided.

"Miss Hinson," he greeted her with a nod. "I know I'm early but I was ready so I thought I'd come and see if I could help."

"I've already put the meat on the grill and the vegetables will go on soon. All I have to do is go in and make the salad."

"Let me do that. I could always make a mean salad," he laughed.

"Well, if you insist. Come on in." She led the way into the kitchen.

In the kitchen, Callie set out the salad makings while he rinsed his hands. She watched as he tore the lettuce and made each of them a delicious looking salad.

"Why did you tear the lettuce instead of cutting it?"

"They tell me, Miss Hinson, that tearing the lettuce is better because it separates naturally cell-wise and cutting it slices through the cells. Maybe it's less painful if it's torn," he teased.

Out of the Darkness

"You could be right," she laughed with him. "Pretty salads."

"And they're going to taste good, too." He reached into the back pocket of his jeans and held up a clear glass bottle of salad dressing.

"Did you make that?" She reached and lifted the cap and smelled it. "Oh, wow! This smells delicious.

"Yes, I made it. I got the ingredients when I was in town. It's my favorite dressing. I learned to make it from my mother."

"I can't wait to eat it. Are you going to share the recipe?" she asked.

He flashed her a sly grin and didn't say a word for a full minute. "Probably not," he finally answered.

"I expected that. You, Marc Reed, are a mystery, so your salad dressing may as well be a mystery, too."

"I'm not a mystery, ma'am. Not really. I'm just at a cross roads in a lot of ways. I'm trying to find my way, I think," he said quietly.

Callie watched him struggle with his words and she could feel his uneasiness. "I truly hope you find your way, Marc. I hope you find what you're looking for."

"Thank you, Miss Hinson, I appreciate that."

"My name is Callie Hinson, but you can call me Callie," she commented, teasingly.

He caught her meaning and laughed out loud. "All right, Miss Hinson. Callie it is," he teased right back at her.

When Tom Hinson returned to the patio, he found the two young people working side by side getting the food prepared and moving it to the picnic table.

"Oh, this looks delicious. I always enjoy eating here on the patio. Callie, do you remember how your mom would serve us dinner out here?"

"I sure do, Dad. Mom could make a sandwich seem like a party," she reminisced.

"Yes, she certainly could. Man, I miss her."

Callie reached across the table and touched his hand. "I know, Dad. I miss her, too. At least she's not sick anymore."

"You're right. That's the only thing that gets me through sometimes," he admitted.

"One day, Dad. We'll see her again and Dirk, too. They're going to be so glad to see us," her smile was growing teary.

The guest at their table listened quietly to the conversation between Tom Hinson and his daughter. It was evident that he had no idea what they were talking about, but he was too polite to question the private conversation going on around him.

Tom Hinson sighed deeply as if to end the serious dialogue he'd just had with daughter. "Everybody ready to pray?" He held out one hand to his daughter and the other to the man seated on his right.

The conversation was light and friendly as the trio sat and ate their meal. The topics ranged from the gathering of the remaining crops, to Lizzie's baby, to Callie's shop in town.

"Dad, it's time to renew the contract on my shop. Mr. Randall dropped the contract by for me to read and sign. I looked over it and I don't see any changes. Do you think I need to go ahead and sign it or do you want to look it over first?"

"I don't think Bob Randall would try to cheat you, Callie. You've rented that building for nearly six years now without any problems."

"Callie, if I might say so, don't ever sign any contract without taking it to an attorney first. Clauses or stipulations can be added that could cause you giant headaches later," Marc advised.

"Yeah, I guess you're right. I'll call Mr. Thomas tomorrow and get an appointment," she agreed.

"I've...I've had some law training. I'd be glad to look at the contract for you," he offered.

"Really! I have it in my work bag. After we finish eating, I'll get it and you can take a look at it," Callie exclaimed.

Out of the Darkness

Tom Hinson looked at the young man sitting at his table. "Son, do you mean to tell me that you're trained in the law? Why on earth would you be sleeping in a tent and working on a farm?"

Marc looked uncomfortably at Callie and then at her father, as they were both staring at him. "Well, Sir, I don't have an answer to your questions. I guess I just need you to trust me," he finally answered.

"But, Marc, if you're a lawyer, you need to be practicing law, not pitching hay bales," the older man argued.

"I don't expect either of you to understand, but I'm doing exactly what I need to be doing," he explained the best he could.

A lengthy pause stretched around the table, then Callie broke the silence. "Well, Marc, there's a lot we don't know about you. Myself, I don't know if you are a lawyer or a farmer. I don't know why you are camping in the woods. But there's one thing I'm sure about...is this dressing of yours! This stuff is amazing!" she exclaimed.

The two men stared at her while she continued to stab her salad with her fork. They looked at each other and had to laugh at Callie and her off the cuff remark.

After Marc's bombshell, somehow the atmosphere, as well as the conversation got back to normal, almost. Callie brought her contract to Marc, and he quietly read through the two page document.

He slipped the contract back into its envelope and handed it back to Callie. "It looks good. No ultimatums or stipulations."

"Thank you, Marc. So you think it's okay for me to sign it?"

"I do. It's a simple, straight-forward contract. As long as you pay your rent, you can't be evicted," he summed up the situation.

She signed the contract and sighed. "At least I have my shop for another year," she voiced her thoughts.

"That's good, Callie," her dad answered, then stood up. "I'm going to check on Lizzie's baby. That little rascal is some kind of houdini. He escapes, then Lizzie goes wild." He took off for the barn and Callie watched him leave.

"Don't you want to go with him, Marc?" She asked, hoping he would go.

"No. I'd rather help you carry these dishes inside and, maybe, answer some of the questions you have buzzing around inside your head," he grinned.

They carried the dishes to the kitchen and Callie ran a sink full of hot water. "Most of the dishes go into the dishwasher but I don't put my knives or plastics in there. I wash them by hand." Callie searched for something to say.

"Come on, Callie. Let me have it. I know you've got to be mad because I didn't tell you when I first came that I'm an attorney."

"No," she refuted him. "I'm not mad. Actually it explains a lot of things that I just couldn't figure out."

"Such as?"

"Well for starters, now I know how you got your expensive vehicle. I can also stop wondering about your nice clothes, your fancy watch, and those designer sunglasses," she replied.

"You wondered about those things?"

"Marc," she stressed, "it's not everyday that a person takes up residence in someone's woods while he dresses like he should be on Wall Street," she laughed.

"I guess I didn't think that through," he admitted. "I didn't plan on running into people as nice as you and your dad."

"Oh, you just think we're nice because we feed you," she teased.

"Well, I admit, that doesn't hurt my cause," he teased right back.

"We don't want you to starve in our woods," she laughed. "But we still don't know very much about you. In the five weeks that you've been here, we know your name and vocation. And that's all."

"I'm sure you're wondering where I'm from and why I'm here," he said quietly.

Out of the Darkness

"I'm trying to stay out of your business," she eyed him. "I keep myself busy and try to let everyone else do the same."

"I know that. Actually it surprises me that you don't ask more questions."

"Like I said," Callie repeated, "it's none of my business."

"Okay, forget about me. May I ask you some questions?"

"Me?" she asked in surprise. "What do you want to ask me?"

"Okay, but don't be mad," he warned.

"All right," she agreed.

"Callie, why is it you've never married?"

Surprised, again, at his straight forward question. She started to ignore the question, then changed her mind. "Boy, you don't beat around the bush, do you?"

"I'm sorry. I shouldn't have asked that," he apologized.

"No, you shouldn't have."

"No answers?" he pressed.

"Not on your life," she answered testily. "You see, Mr. Reed, you're not the only one that can keep his cards close to the vest."

"I asked for that. I'm sorry, Callie," he repeated.

She turned back to the sink without a word.

"Callie, look at me. Please," he urged.

She turned to look at him questioningly.

"I won't ask anything personal again. I promise. Okay?" he vowed.

"Okay."

"Look, I do have some serious questions that I'd like to talk to you about," he ventured.

"All right. Go ahead," she sighed.

"Your mom died when you were a young girl, isn't that right?" he asked.

41

"Yes. I was twelve. She died with cancer," she informed him.

"Callie, I just heard you and your dad talking about her and how you would see her again. What did you mean?" he asked in confusion.

"Well, Marc, we know we'll see her again. She's in heaven and we're going there," she assured him.

"I'm not trying to be contradictory, but, Callie, how can that be?"

"It will happen because my mom was a Christian. Dad and I are Christians, too, so that's how we know," she explained.

"But...I..., exactly what does it mean when you say you're a Christian? Does it mean you go to church?"

"Well, we do go to church but that's not what makes us a Christian. When I was eleven years old, I realized I was a sinner and I asked Jesus into my heart to save me and be my Savior. That day I became a child of God. And *that's* what makes me a Christian," she finished.

"Your mom and dad did the same thing? Asked Jesus into their hearts like you did, I mean?"

"Yep. They were Christians before I was born," she commented.

"I don't understand this sinner part. I doubt an eleven year old girl was a very bad person," he reasoned.

"Oh, I hadn't robbed any banks, that's true, but I was born a sinner. We all are. That's why Jesus came to earth as a baby, grew up, and died on the cross for our sins. Anyone that will come to him and earnestly seek his forgiveness for all the bad things we do or even think, He forgives us and we become His child," she finished.

"I've never heard it put quite so plainly before," he stated.

"Didn't you go to church, Marc, before you came here, I mean?"

"No. Not regularly, that is. I guess I didn't see the need," he admitted.

"We all have that need, Marc," she commented without judgment.

"I'm beginning to see that. What if He doesn't want some of us?" he asked.

"There's not one that He doesn't love or want," she smiled.

"I wish I could be sure of that," he stated.

"That's where faith comes in."

"Sometime I come up here and your dad will be reading his Bible. Do you read your Bible, too?" he questioned.

"Everyday! That's God's Word to us."

"It brings you happiness, doesn't it?" he wondered.

"Well, not exactly. Happiness depends on happenings. My Bible brings me joy. Things can fall apart all around me and I might be crying a bucket of tears, but I still have joy in my heart because God is with me and I know it," she smiled.

"I wish I could say that. In my world when things are falling apart, I'm falling apart, too," he admitted.

Callie studied the man that had just bared his heart to her and decided she, nor he, didn't have anything to lose.

"Tomorrow's Sunday. Why don't you go to church with us?" she invited.

"I don't know, Callie. For starters, the roof would probably cave in on me," he tried to joke.

"Oh, I doubt that. I don't think you're such a hard case."

"I'll think about it," he answered.

After he went back to his campsite, Callie couldn't dismiss their conversation. There were many things about him that she did not know, but nothing was as important as Marc becoming a Christian. Her prayer for the rest of the day would be for her neighbor. Whatever he needs, her prayer was that he would find it.

Chapter 8

On Sunday morning, Callie prayed that Mark would join them at church. When they arrived, she looked for his black SUV among the cars in the parking lot but it wasn't there. She even looked up and down the street, but Marc's vehicle was nowhere to be seen.

Even though she was disappointed, she was more determined than ever to keep praying for him. It was evident his life was filled with loose ends, but she knew that God was the only one to bring his life together.

At home, the aroma of her Sunday dinner greeted her as soon as she opened the door. The bar-b-que in the slow cooker was ready to eat, and she added a couple of side dishes she had picked up at the supermarket on the way home.

When the meal was on the table, she wondered what Marc was having for his Sunday meal. Callie had made extra just in case he decided to join them. When he didn't, she made up a plate.

"Dad, do you want to take this food to Marc?"

"Sure, Honey. Let me change my clothes. This is not the attire to wear to the woods," he laughed.

Callie cleared the table as she heard her dad's ATV leave the driveway. Sunday afternoons were prime time for a nap, but today she didn't feel like sleeping. Instead, she went to the back patio and sat in her mother's favorite place. She had a perfect view of the blooming fall flowers, as well as the fields which were beginning to lose their bright green hue. Her mom had solved many problems by sitting on the bench and talking things over with the Lord. More and more, Callie found herself going to her mother's bench.

Why did she feel the need to come to the Lord so often? Her business was a success; the contract on her salon had been secured for another year. Her dad was slowing down some, she had noticed, but he was still active and in good health. The only thing she was uneasy about was Marc.

It didn't matter to her anymore about his past. Where he had come from and why he was living in their woods was no longer important. But what did matter was the fact that he wasn't a Christian. His law degree had bought him an expensive car and many other benefits, but without Christ, he was as poor as a pauper.

She was brought out of her mind wandering by the sound of her dad's return on the ATV. Immediately, she recognized, by the loudness, there was more than one four-wheeler in the driveway.

When Marc came sauntering around the corner of the house, she was not surprised.

"Callie, may I join you or is this a private meeting?" he asked quietly.

"Sure. Have a seat."

"I'm sorry about this morning. I chickened out. I fully intended to come, but I started thinking about walking into a church full of strangers.... and I just couldn't do it," he explained.

"Hey, Marc, it's totally okay. I understand."

"I didn't want to disappoint you," he admitted.

"You didn't disappoint me," she responded. "You don't owe me anything."

"But, I do! You've invested a lot of time and conversation in me and my troubles," he laughed lightly.

"No, that's not so," she laughed.

"Well, anyway, I wanted to apologize," he repeated.

"Not a problem. Although, we had a great service. I wish you had been there. You might understand a little more of how God loves us, you included."

"I know what you tell me, but I don't understand how he could love me. I've never been a faithful church goer. To be honest, I've never given God much thought at all," he revealed.

"Okay, tell me something, Marc. Do you believe in God?"

"Sure! I'm not an atheist, if that's what you mean," he answered. "I know there is a God."

"Well, that's a start."

"Oh, Callie," he sighed. "It's easy for you to believe. I mean, look at your life. You've lived right here in this little town where the people are decent, loving people. You've not lived the way I've lived or seen what I've seen."

"I admit, I've lived a pretty protected life, and I'm thankful to call this place home," she responded.

"I'm glad for the life you've lived. The only child of loving parents has got to be wonderful," he surmised.

"But, I'm not an only child," she corrected him.

"Really? I thought...I didn't know you had any siblings," he exclaimed.

"I do. I have a brother in heaven."

"Do you mean your brother died?"

"Yes. Dirk was three years older than me. When he was thirteen and I was ten, he got very sick. He had acute leukemia. He got sick and within three weeks, he was gone." Her voice grew quiet.

"I'm so sorry, Callie. I had no idea," he sympathized.

"Well, it has been a long time now," she paused....."You know what, Marc? I've never told anyone this, but I've always felt guilty about being alive and my brother being dead. I feel that my parents were cheated. They got stuck with me while they lost their son. Dirk was such a good person. He was so kind and helpful to everyone, especially to me. He was so patient with me. He taught me to ride a bicycle and to ride his horse named Pete. Dirk loved the farm. All he ever wanted to do was to work with dad on this farm, but that wasn't meant to be. I don't think mom ever got over losing Dirk. Two years later, she was gone, too. Poor dad, here he was left with a twelve year old daughter instead of a young farmer son," she remarked.

He sat quietly listening, then softly commented, "Callie, I don't think any of what you're feeling is true. Of course, I never knew your mother or your brother, but I feel confident that they wouldn't want you to feel this way."

"I don't know about that. I can only imagine how dad missed... misses both of them. You know, Marc, I think that's partly why he loves having you around so much," she confided to him.

"I doubt that," he laughed. "I'm not very proficient around the farm. He taught me to drive a tractor and how to pitch a bale of hay without breaking my back or strewing hay everywhere. And so many more things," he added.

"Well, it is what it is." She handed off the old cliché with a half smile.

"Is this why you've stayed in your home town and lived at home? To help your dad, I mean?"

"Partly," she admitted, "but, I genuinely love this town. I love Hannah at the diner and Mr. Rhodes at the service station. Mr. Graham, the president of our bank, knows everyone that comes through those doors. I know all the clerks at the supermarket and they know me. It's the same with all the other business establishments. We know each other, we love each other, and we help each other when it's needed."

"I, for one, think you have a good life here in this town. But..., Callie, I've been here six weeks and I haven't heard one word about a boyfriend. Is he a secret or is he MIA?"

Callie couldn't help her reaction to his inquisitiveness, she laughed out loud. "Marc, if you only knew how I have had to bob and weave from all the people that keep trying to find me a boyfriend. I mean, it's constant. You should hear the ladies at my shop that want to introduce me to their nephew, or their cousin's handsome, unattached son," she rolled her eyes. Turning to him, she had her own questions.

"Okay, Mr. Attorney, it's your turn to be interrogated. You've already said you didn't leave behind a wife. How about a girlfriend?"

"No. No girlfriend," he answered.

"How old are you, Marc?"

"I'm thirty-one."

"Don't you want to go home and find a nice girl, get married and raise a family?"

"Yes, Callie, I do. But at the present time, I don't even know where to call home. I'm feeling more at home right here than I did in my home town," he admitted.

"You can always find some place around our town and settle down."

"Believe me, I've thought about it. I even drove around town looking in yards trying to find for sale signs. But, that's not practical while I've still got so many questions that need answers and decisions to be made," he declared.

"Well, I can't tell you what to do, but I can pray for you."

He quickly looked her way and held her gaze. "I would appreciate that, Callie. I don't know which way to turn. I want to forget my past and start over in this little town, but then, I don't know if that would be the right thing to do. My parents love me, yet I'm rather estranged from them. We haven't had words or an argument of any kind but I don't feel I can go back home. Not yet, at least," he added.

"Oh, Marc, don't put it off too long. You only have one mom and dad," she reminded him.

"Do you want me to leave, Callie?"

"Well, no. But that's up to you. I mean, you're the only one that can make that decision. You have to take all things into consideration. Your parents, their health and happiness, plus your career. Do you want to go back to your old job or start over in a new place?" She laid it out before him.

"I appreciate your advice. You're right, you know. I can go back, but I'm not ready. I think I could use some of those prayers you were talking about earlier."

Out of the Darkness

"That I can do," she promised. "You know, Marc, it's more than making a decision about going back to where you came from. It's about your life. You can go home right now, today, but you would be going home, taking all of your indecisions with you. I'm afraid you would probably take off again to someone else's woods." She let a small smile capture her lips.

He laughed with her. "You're right again."

"I thought so," she laughed, "but I can still pray for you."

"I would like that."

Callie felt a seriousness from him and vowed to herself to not neglect praying for him.

Chapter 9

The next three days when Callie got home from work, Marc was at the farm helping her dad. The two men enjoyed a healthy camaraderie between them. She prayed that their friendship would lead to the younger man confiding in her dad. She could talk to him and pray for him, but she felt her dad's years of experience and wisdom could be valuable help to someone drifting in every aspect of his life.

Since Marc refused to take wages for his work on the farm, Tom Hinson insisted that the younger man eat the evening meal with him and his daughter. Callie was growing accustomed to having an extra for dinner and planned accordingly. Each night, she discreetly observed their guest as he ate. He was becoming more relaxed as the days went by. When he first came to their woods, weeks before, he was quiet, even withdrawn and polite. Now he talked more than anyone else at the table. He told funny stories, mostly on himself, about his learning the ways of the farm. Most nights, he insisted on helping Callie with the clean up, while teasing in a friendly, pleasant way.

This night when the kitchen was in order, Marc was in no hurry to go back to his camp. Callie wondered why he was hesitating, because he usually shot for the door like a bullet when dinner was over and the table cleared.

Callie left the two men in friendly conversation in the living room and went about her business of preparing for the next day's work. She was folding a load of towels when Marc appeared at the laundry room door.

"Callie? Is there anything I can do to help?"

Out of the Darkness

"Oh, no. Thank you. I'm about finished here. Besides, you've worked hard today. You need to put your feet up and relax," she instructed him.

"You've worked all day, too, and on your feet, I might add. Let me help," he insisted.

"Okay, be my guest." She moved to give him room at the folding table. He followed her lead and wrestled with bringing the bath towels into a tight roll. He folded and refolded his towel until he finally produced a passable rolled up towel.

The pile of linens shrank quickly with both Callie and Marc working on them.

"Thank you for your help," Callie commented when the table was empty.

"You are welcome, and thank you for dinner...again," he laughed. "Everyday I promise myself that I won't bother you folks but it seems I can't stay away. I love being with your dad. He's so easy to talk to. Then, I find myself waiting around so I can see you."

"I have to say, you're not very choosy," she laughed. "Dinner, as you call it, is either something from Hannah's or something cooked to death in a slow cooker."

"Now, that's not true, You cook some pretty tasty quisine in the slow cooker," he laughed with her. "But, it may not be the food alone. Maybe it's the company I find here."

"Whatever it is, Marc, you are welcome here. My dad thinks the world of you," she commented.

"And you?" he questioned, giving her a sideways look.

"I don't count."

"Oh, but you do. I like you, Callie. You are so easy to talk to. You're a hard worker. You never complain. After working all day, you come home, make dinner and even welcome a near stranger to your table. Your quite a girl, Callie Hinson, and a pretty one at that," he added.

She stared at him while he made his flowery speech. "You just haven't been around a girl in a while, have you, Mr. Attorney?" she teased.

51

Debrah Gish

He had to laugh at her quick wit. "And another thing, Callie, you can think on your feet. There's not much that gets by you, I can tell."

"Well, I may be dumb but I'm not stupid," she declared.

"There's not one dumb or stupid bone in your body," he insisted. "On that note, I'm going back to the woods."

"Marc, do you have enough blankets to stay warm? The temperature is starting to fall at night."

"I do. I think my sleeping bag is guaranteed to withstand thirty-five degrees below zero," he laughed.

"Well, I believe you're safe for a while," she teased, "but if you get cold, I can send more blankets."

"Thanks, Callie, I'll keep that in mind."

"Marc....I've seen your shower," she mentioned awkwardly. "It's too cool to shower outside. Why don't you use our shower here in the house."

"I don't want to be a bother."

"All right, if you won't use the shower here in the house, why don't you use the shower in dad's office in the barn. At least it's heated."

"Your dad has been trying to get me to use his office, too. I don't know, Callie, I hate to inconvenience people."

"Marc, you're not causing an inconvenience. You help dad everyday, and without pay, I might add. Let us help you that much, at least," Callie insisted.

"I'll seriously think about it."

"And, Marc," she patted the washer behind her, "these machines are at your disposal."

"Do you mean, 'Make myself at home'?"

"Exactly," she agreed. "It's soon going to get very cold here in Michigan. We don't want our nearest neighbor turning into an icicle. You need good warm showers at the end of the day, then you need warm clean clothes to keep you from getting sick."

"I'll try to stay warm and healthy," he stated. With that remark he waved a short goodbye and left the house.

Long after Callie had turned in for the night, she prayed for Marc. She prayed for his safety during the night and she prayed for his lost way. He was directionless and she felt that would be a terrible place to be.

In such a small town as hers, Callie found it hard to believe that not one of her customers had mentioned the man staying in the woods just outside of town. One thing Callie knew; if her customers knew about Marc, he would be the daily topic in her beauty salon. A young, handsome, unattached man would be the talk of the town. So, she was positive his presence was still a secret, but for how long, she wasn't sure.

Two days later when she arrived home from work, she found the kitchen occupied with the two men preparing dinner. Her dad was never one to cook so she was not surprised to see Marc with a towel wrapped around him apron style, busy at the stove. Whatever he was cooking smelled delicious and she didn't try to hide her curiosity.

"What in the world is that wonderful smell?" She went straight to the stove and started lifting lids.

"It's my mom's curried chicken with veggies," he answered.

"Oh, it smells amazing!"

"Here try it." Marc took a spoon from the drawer, scooped up a spoonful, and blew on it. "Open up."

Callie opened to the full spoon and closed her eyes in response. "Oh, Wow! That's delicious."

"It's ready. Why don't you shed your coat and we'll eat," he commented.

When they were seated and Tom Hinson had prayed, Marc filled Callie's plate with rice smothered with chicken in a curried sauce that contained tiny broccoli florets.

"Thank you, Marc! This looks scrumptious and has the house smelling wonderful! This is quite a treat," she admitted. "Thank you."

"Tom and I thought we'd give you a night off. You come in everyday and put a hot meal on the table."

"Well, not every night," she confessed. "Some nights it's Hannah's Diner that feeds us."

"It doesn't matter who cooks it. You make the meal come together," he insisted. Then he added, "And, Miss Callie, I showered in the barn office. I hope you are satisfied," he taunted with a grin.

"Well, I must say that I am glad to hear that," she answered with a hint of sass in her voice.

"I'm trying to get him to move into the office. It's warm and would be much more comfortable," her dad entered the conversation.

From across the table, Callie watched the two men as they went back and forth.

"Now, Tom, you know we've been all through this before."

"But, Marc, it's going to get very cold this winter. We have big snows in this part of the country," Tom Hinson insisted.

"Dad, Marc may not even be here this winter."

At her remark, Marc caught her gaze and held it. Then he commented, "She's right, Tom, I don't know how long I'll be here."

"Of course, it's your decision," the older man conceded, "but you're welcome here as long as you want to stay."

"Thank you, Tom, I appreciate that."

Callie kept her silence. As far as she was concerned, she still expected him to load up and pull out of their woods and their lives just any day. That was not her worry, but his spiritual condition or lack thereof was troubling to her. She really wanted him to settle things with God. Without that relationship, his life was never going to come together.

"More chicken and rice, Callie?"

In surprise, Callie brought her focus back to the present. "Uh...yes, please, but just a little." She held her plate for the refill. "This is delicious, Marc. My compliments to your mom."

"I will tell her when I talk to her," he replied.

"You talk to her?" Callie asked in surprise.

"Yes, Ma'am, every Saturday."

His answer gave her plenty to think about. Who is this man that prepared this delicious meal? He apparently loved his mother, so why did he run away from her and stay away so long? He had now been a squatter in their woods for many weeks. Still, all they knew about him was his name and his profession. Why did he leave home and what was keeping him here?

While her mind was mulling over Marc and his mysteries, she missed the first part of her dad's conversation, but her ears suddenly picked up what he was saying.

…. "we'll be starting early and working until late. Are you sure you want to do this?"

"Of course. I'm not scared of hard work, Tom. I'll be ready. What time do you want me here?"

"Wait! What are you two talking about?" Callie asked, being totally oblivious as to what they were discussing.

"I'm going to help your dad get the crops in. I know there are two other guys that help, but I can help, too."

"But, Marc, are you sure? Sometime the days can be twelve to sixteen hours long. Harvesting can last three weeks or longer. Are you sure you want to do this?"

"Yes, I'm sure. I said I want to help and I will," he replied rather sternly.

"Well, okay. You're going to be completely exhausted at the end of every day," she warned.

"I know."

"You'll need your rest," she added.

"Umhum," he agreed.

Callie stared at him, then turned to her dad. "If he is going to help with the crops, you have to get him to move into that office."

"Well, I've been trying to talk him into it. I told him we'd put a bed in there for him."

"Marc, you need to move from your tent into Dad's office. At least while you're helping day and night with the crops," she argued.

"Now, Callie."

"No, Marc. It's just sensible. We have extra beds in this house." She turned to her dad. "Dad, we have twin beds in Dirk's room. He only slept in one. The other was never used unless one of his friends stayed over. We can move that bed to the office. Okay?"

"Well, of course. Callie, that's an excellent idea," he answered thoughtfully.

"Let's finish our meal, then you two can move the bed to the barn tonight," she instructed. "And Marc, you can move in when you're ready."

"Are you sure about this, Callie?" Marc questioned.

"Yes, I am," she answered firmly, as if to close the subject.

True to her word, Callie led the way down the hall and opened the bedroom door that was always kept closed. The room was spotless, not a piece of clutter or a speck of dust could be found. The room, though unoccupied, was exactly like her brother had left it, fifteen years before. Callie stripped the bed of its sheets and comforter so the men could dismantle the frame and carry it to the barn. She followed them out of the bedroom, stopping only to take fresh sheets and a blanket from the linen closet.

The barn office was big enough for a desk and the twin bed, but not much else. Callie went back to the house and took an occasional table from her own bedroom and carried it across the yard to the barn. A small armless chair was used only to hold unread magazines, so Callie moved the magazines to a shelf and moved the chair closer to the bed.

"Now," she exclaimed, looking around the room," you have a bed, a table, a chair, and a bathroom," she pointed to the narrow door behind them. "Anything else you need?"

"I believe you've covered it all. Even made up my bed," he said, pointing to the neatly made bed.

"I'm sorry." Callie was embarrassed and apologized. "I guess I got carried away."

"Well, thank you, Callie. Your help is much appreciated," Marc responded.

Callie knew his appreciation was more of a tease than anything else and it slightly irritated her.

"Goodnight, you two," she commented and left them alone to make their plans for the next day.

Even though she knew they didn't expect her to make breakfast, Callie knew she would not let her dad leave for the fields without a nourishing breakfast. If she had to feed Marc, too, well, that couldn't be helped. She wrestled with the thought of Marc living in the barn. She was troubled at the idea that her dad was so fond of the man. She knew, one day when he loaded up his expensive car and drove away, that her dad would feel the loss greatly.

Chapter 10

Early the next morning, as soon her alarm sounded, Callie was up, dressed and in the kitchen. She had a breakfast of eggs, bacon, and hot biscuits, along with fresh coffee, ready for the table when her dad put in an appearance in the kitchen.

"Now, Callie, Honey, you don't need to cook breakfast for me. I can eat a couple cookies and a cup of coffee, you know that."

Ignoring his protest, Callie motioned toward the door, "Go get your neighbor. I'll have breakfast on the table when you get back."

He left and came back quickly with Marc close behind him.

"Sit down, guys, and eat. The day's awastin'," she teased.

Without a word they sat down and looked at Callie to join them.

"I'll just have coffee," she held up her over-sized mug. "I'm going to get ready for work."

Shortly, she returned to find the kitchen empty and the dishes in the sink. She rinsed them and loaded the dishwasher.

On the way to work, she whispered a prayer for her dad and his helpers for their safety. Farming accidents happen everyday and she was always fearful of getting that kind of call. As she prayed, she wondered how Marc had made his way into her prayers lately, but there he was.

Her day was busy and that kept her mind occupied instead of fretting about how the harvest was going. Hopefully none of the equipment would break down. Equipment failure could delay the crop gathering for days, even weeks. Her dad was always stressed during harvest season; she didn't figure this year would be any different.

Callie thought over her role in the farming and decided she could send them off with a good breakfast but would let Hannah's Diner feed them dinner.

It was already dark when she arrived home with their dinner. The lights were all on in the barn and the tractor shed but she suspected the men were still in the fields.

An hour later, she decided to eat her dinner and put the other containers in the microwave. Callie had just opened her styrofoam lid when her dad came in the door.

Rising from her chair, Callie said, "Hey, Dad, let me get your dinner." She looked behind him. "Where's Marc?"

"He said he didn't want to trouble you. So, I think he's going to the campsite to fix himself something to eat."

"Well....of all things," Callie sputtered and took off out the door. At the barn, she called his name.

"Marc."

"Callie? What are you doing out here?" He came out of the office drying his hands and face on a towel.

"I came to get you for dinner."

"Now, you don't have to feed me."

"I know that, but you're helping my dad and I appreciate it. So, come and eat with us," she urged.

"Callie, I'm not a moocher. I don't feel right about you doing so much for me."

"Well, I didn't cook dinner tonight. Hannah did," she laughed.

"Well, I guess, in that case, I need to come to the house for dinner," he joined her laughter.

Together they walked to the house where Tom Hinson was waiting for the young folks to come and eat with him.

They ate mostly in silence, with Callie doing the majority of the talking. She was mildly amused when both men left the table and went in opposite directions. Her dad headed straight down the hall to get a shower and she suspected Marc was headed to his room in the barn for the same purpose. She had to admit, the two bright and cheery men that she'd left that morning had little resemblance to the two worn out farmers that just had dinner with her. She tidied the kitchen and went to bed herself. The alarm clock was set so she could again send the odd couple off to the fields in a few short hours.

Just as Callie suspected, the next morning, both men appeared at her breakfast table, looking fresh and rested.

She went to her salon knowing that her day was filled with appointments. Early in the day, she called the diner and ordered dinner. When her last appointment left, Callie quickly closed her shop and drove to the diner to collect her order.

Again, the house was dark but she soon had the lights on and dinner in the warm oven to wait for the two farmers that would soon be coming.

They arrived shortly, looking totally exhausted. They took turns washing up in the half bath just down the hall. They ate with few words and just like the night before, they left the kitchen to go in opposite directions. Callie cleared the table, but her mind was on her dad. He looked exhausted. She prayed he was not pushing himself too hard. Sure, Marc was working the long hours along side her dad, but his youth and strength made him more able to withstand the long days.

The entire week was spent in long days of farm work and Callie looked forward to the weekend. Hopefully, the men would take Sunday to rest but she wasn't sure if they could or would. Farmers usually worked day and night, seven days a week during crop gathering time and that's what she expected to happen this time, also.

On Saturday, her work ended shortly after noon. She stopped by the supermarket for groceries then drove home. She put away her purchases before changing out of her uniform and diving into her housework. Within two hours, the house was shining and she had laid out what she was preparing for dinner.

With a short window of time left before preparing dinner, Callie took her Bible and went to the yard swing on the back patio. She took a few minutes to enjoy her peaceful surroundings. The birds were enjoying the tall beautiful trees that her mother loved so much. The leaves were turning and added to the beauty. Callie closed her eyes and listened to the world around her. The distant hum of farm machinery couldn't drown out the peace of her happy place.

Contented, she opened her Bible and read several chapters in Psalms. Of course, she finished her devotions by reading Psalm twenty-three, her favorite Bible passage. *The Lord is my Shepherd.....*she smiled at the thought. Her life was good. She was happy. She had a good home. Her health was good. She loved her job. She wasn't wealthy, but her bank account was in good shape.

Yet, with all the positives in her life, she had questions. She was twenty-five years old and lived with her aging father. She took care of the house and meals as if it was her own home. Her question....why wasn't she unhappy? She had no man in her life at the present but she was fine with that. She loved her small town and couldn't imagine living anywhere else. Even if it meant living her life alone.

With a long sigh, she hugged her Bible close to her chest and spoke out loud. *"Lord, this is too big for me. You're going to have to handle this part of my life."*

It was long past dark when the men came inside to eat. They brightened up slightly when they saw the delicious dinner that Callie had prepared for them.

While they enjoyed the still warm apple pie, topped with vanilla ice cream, Tom Hinson made an announcement. "Now, Marc, tomorrow we're going to take the day off."

"Are you sure, Tom?" Marc asked in surprise. "We can get a lot done in a day, you know."

"That's true, my boy," he agreed, "but I've decided, if we can't get it done in six days, we can't get it done in seven. Tomorrow is the Lord's Day and a day of rest for us and we're going to take it."

Callie silently watched her dad as he quietly made decisions for himself and the younger man beside him. Marc nodded his head in agreement as if he understood but Callie suspected he didn't have a clue about what her dad was talking about. She was still praying for him and hopefully, one day, he would understand.

Chapter 11

Callie was up early on Sunday morning and cooked breakfast for herself and her dad. She was sure their borrowed help would still be sleeping, so she decided not to bother him with breakfast.

She was almost ready for church when she heard her dad talking in the living room. Thinking he was on the telephone, she avoided the living room and collected her coat, purse, and Bible. She and her dad usually drove separately to church, just in case Callie needed to stop by her shop or by the market. On her way out, she stopped to tell her dad she was leaving. She entered the room but was stopped by the sight of the man beside her father.

Her mouth flew open at the sight of Marc dressed in a two piece navy suit, white shirt and tie. His shiny leather shoes showed no sign of him living in a make shift bedroom in the corner of a barn.

"Marc....how...where..," she stammered.

He laughed at her confusion.

"Are you wanting to know how I could clean up and look presentable?" he asked, still laughing.

"Yeah, I guess so."

"Well, I do have dress clothes," he joked. "I don't always wear jeans."

"I must say, you clean up pretty good. I'm impressed," she half joked but was more serious than she liked.

He just gave her that half smile, but she had more questions.

"What are you doing all dressed up?"

"I thought I'd accompany the two of you to church," he stated. "I assume it's okay?"

"Well, of course it is." She turned to her dad, "I'm going on. I'll see you there." For some reason, she wanted to escape from Marc. He looked totally different than when he wore jeans and a flannel shirt. She could talk to the farmer Marc, but the lawyer, she wasn't so sure.

The ten minute trip to church was spent entirely on the fact that Marc would be coming to church this morning. She knew everyone would be curious about the visitor but she didn't care. Marc's life was still unsettled and she knew he was looking for help. Hopefully he would get some answers for his life this morning, or at least start on the journey that could lead to some clarification for him.

Callie waited in the church parking lot for her dad's truck to arrive so they could all walk into church together. She was surprised to see Marc's SUV pull in with her dad riding in the passenger's seat.

They parked next to Callie and she joined them. They went into the church with her dad leading the way. When they stopped at their usual pew, Callie was careful to make sure her dad sat in the middle.

Friends and neighbors came by to welcome the new visitor. Tom Hinson was quick to introduce Marc Reed as someone who was helping out on the farm.

Callie hoped she looked more comfortable than she felt as she smiled at her church family. She tried her best to keep her attention focused away from the handsome man seated on the other side of her dad. One thing she definitely didn't want was folks getting ideas about her and the new farm hand. True, he was pleasant, dressed nice and looked every bit the lawyer she knew him to be. Still, their small town, along with the people in it, was just a stop gap for Marc.

When he figured out his dilemma, whatever it was, he would load up and leave. When that day came, Callie intended he go back with what he had brought and not one thing more. Mainly, she determined her heart would be left as it was right now. Peaceful and unattached.

As the music started, people found their places and Callie could relax. Out of the corner of her eye, she watched Marc fumble with his song book. It was evident he was lost in the songs. The pastor went to the pulpit and Tom Hinson shared his Bible with his visitor.

The message was a clear salvation message and Callie prayed through the entire sermon that Marc might hear something that he could take to his heart.

After the last prayer, the trio filed out with the rest of the congregation. Callie started for her car but was stopped by Marc.

"Why don't the three of us go somewhere and have lunch? I'm buying. After all, you've fed me all week."

"You and dad go. I'm sure there's farm plans you need to discuss," Callie declined.

"No, we don't," her dad spoke up. "I'm going home and make myself a big ham sandwich with that ham you baked yesterday. Then, there's a recliner with my name on it. I'm going to nap until bedtime, then I'm going to bed," he laughed. "Callie, you go with Marc. Take him to that burger place that we all rave about. While you're at it, show him our covered bridges," he instructed.

"Dad, Marc doesn't want a burger from Bea's Drive-in and I'm sure he's seen his share of covered bridges."

"On the contrary, I would love to have one of those famous burgers. Believe it or not, I love covered bridges. I didn't know you had any around here," Marc commented.

"See, Callie," he dad corrected her, "I knew he would. Now run along with him. I'll take your car and go home."

Feeling defeated, Callie handed him her car keys, then turned to Marc.

"I'm sorry you're stuck with me. We'll go get one of those burgers then we'll come right back. It shouldn't take too long."

"I'm not stuck with you," he laughed. "I enjoy your company." He opened the door on his SUV and waited for her to climb inside.

She rolled her eyes at him, stepped up into the vehicle and fastened her seat belt.

He climbed in under the steering wheel and asked, "Okay. Where is this burger place?"

Callie grimaced. "I'm sorry, Marc. It's in the next county. About thirty-five miles from here."

"That's no distance. Just show me where," he said, as he pulled out of the church parking lot.

At home, Callie was on her own turf and conversation came easy but now they were both in strange territory. She had to admit, he was more talkative than she was, but felt he was no more relaxed than she.

At last, the drive-in came into view. Filled with relief, Callie was glad they would have something in their mouths and wouldn't be expected to talk.

"Tell me what to order, Callie." Marc looked over the giant sized menu sign.

"Well, how hungry are you?"

"I'm starving," he laughed.

"Okay, you asked for it," she laughed, and proceeded to order their meal.

She pulled her wallet from her purse and he reacted.

"No, ma'am! Put your money back in your purse, Miss Hinson. You've fed me all week. Now it's my turn."

"But, Marc, you've worked your fingers to the bone this week. We owe you."

"Callie, you have no idea," he stated without any further explanation.

While they waited for their order, Marc shrugged out of his suit coat and slipped off his tie. He laid them carefully in the back seat and Callie could tell he had been taught to be neat. His campsite had been arranged neatly, she recalled. She hadn't seen it, but Callie was pretty sure his room in the barn was kept neat and clean.

When their food came, Marc made a suggestion, "I saw some picnic tables at that little park about a half mile back. Do you think it's too cool to eat outside?"

"No. I don't think so. The sun is really warm today."

At the small picnic area, Marc led them to a table that was in the sun. He dug into the tall, white paper bag and spread their food before them.

Marc bit into his burger while Callie prayed silently before starting on her own sandwich.

After his first bite, he exclaimed, "That's the best burger I have ever eaten! It's delicious!"

"I know, right!" Callie had to laughed.

"Remind me to thank your dad. This burger is amazing!"

"I'm glad you like it," she stated dryly. "Especially since he strong armed you into getting one and dragging me along with you."

"I'm glad he did. I wouldn't want to miss this food for anything," he teased.

They both finished their sandwiches and Marc pushed his remaining fries toward her. "Help me eat these fries."

"I'm sorry. I can't eat another bite," she pushed them back to him.

He paused, started to say something, then paused again. He gave a short laugh.

"You know what? When I was a kid, my brother and I would fight over the leftover fries."

"What!" She exclaimed. "You have a brother? I thought you said you have no siblings."

"Had, is the word. I don't have any siblings living," he explained.

"Oh," she uttered. "I'm sorry."

"Yeah, me, too."

Callie didn't know what to say next. She didn't want Marc to think she didn't care, but on the other hand, she didn't want to pry into his privacy, of which he held onto with all his might. He had been at their farm three months and she was just now hearing about his brother. She decided to let him keep his secrets. If he wanted to share his story with someone, that was his business. If not, she wasn't going to pry.

Callie watched him shift his position, putting his forearms on the table in front of him. When he lifted his head, his eyes were full of misery.

"Callie, I want to tell you about my life. Will you allow me to?"

"Well, of course, but you don't have to, you know."

"I know. I think it's time. I've held everything inside for so long. I'm not sure where to start, so I'm going to start at the beginning. Are you ready?" he tried to tease.

"When you are," she invited him to continue.

It seemed he was gathering his courage and arranging his words but he finally started talking.

"I grew up in a suburb of Columbus, Ohio. My dad is an attorney and my mother is a paralegal. She chose to stay home and raise my brother and me, so she hasn't had a job in my lifetime, except, at times, helping dad with some research. So my home was always normal. Well," he laughed slightly, "as normal as raising two lively boys can make it, I guess. My little brother was almost 6 years younger than me and always such a good kid. When I was growing up, all I ever wanted to be was an attorney, just like my dad. But my little brother had his plans, too. His whole life was preparing to be a soldier. He was just a little guy when he set his sights on being a Marine. My dad and I would sit and watch lawyer and detective shows and Jamey would climb up on the sofa and watch, too, but in his hands, he always had a toy soldier, sometimes two."

Callie listened attentively as he grew more open with his past.

"Jamey never veered off course. I don't know why we didn't see how serious he was about serving his country. We should have paid more attention when he would mention going to the military. That's a failure on me and our dad, but mostly mine. You see, Jamey always looked up to me and I knew it. Surely, I could've changed his mind," he scoffed at himself, then continued.

"I graduated high school, then went to college. I went to law school and passed my bar exam. I moved back home and joined dad's law firm. By that time, Jamey had finished one year at the local community college. He wasn't interested in going away to school. He threw us all for a loop one day when he came home and announced that he'd joined the Marines. All three of us were stunned and tried to talk him out of joining, but he told us he was nineteen years old and had already joined. So, we couldn't do a thing except watch him make his plans and take him to the recruiting office on the appointed day."

"I was busy getting my feet wet in the law firm and loving every minute of it. At this point, I was considering moving out of my parent's house and getting my own place, but I put it off because of my mother. She was so worried about Jamey, and so was dad, that I held off on moving. They missed their youngest so much, and so did I. Well, Jamey went through basic and all was good. After about six months, he landed himself a two week leave and came home. It was so good to see him. I couldn't believe how happy he was. He lived and breathed his military career. When he told us his next orders were for Afghanistan, I thought our mother would faint. Mom and Dad tried to put on a happy front, but I knew they were dying inside. The day he left was a dark day. We had no idea when we would see him again, but we for sure didn't think it would be never," he paused before he picked up where he had left off.

"He sure enough went to the Middle East. He didn't write much but he called when he could get a signal. We face timed at Christmas and on birthdays. Mom sent care packages often filled with Jamey's favorite snacks. I knew they'd be nothing but crumbs by the time they reached him, but she didn't need to know that."

"We didn't hear anything from him for about a week, then one night just as we were about to have dinner, we had company. There at our front door stood two of the finest looking Marines that I had ever seen. Their message broke our hearts. Jamey, our little Jamey, the little boy that clutched those soldier dolls, would not be coming home. He had stepped on a land mine and it literally destroyed him. He came home in a body bag and we couldn't even view him. I was torn up and demanded that they take a DNA sample from me and check it against the person in the flag draped coffin. To my surprise, they complied with my request. When the results were returned, there was no doubt; we had lost Jamey."

"Callie, he was just a kid. He never really got to grow up. He'll never marry and know what it means for someone to commit to loving him forever. He'll never know the joy of having children to call him daddy. He missed out on life, period. He wasn't even twenty-one years old. He lost everything. I had a dream job, good health, and a growing bank account. It just wasn't fair. I couldn't handle it, Callie. I tried. I worked for almost another year, then I fell apart. I went into a dark place that I didn't even know existed. I felt so guilty that Jamey was gone and I was still here. I had no business being alive and healthy. So, I did the only thing I could do. I enlisted in the Marines."

Callie's mouth fell open in surprise at his last statement. "Why Marc?"

"I felt I had to take his place. Secretly, I hoped that I, too, might be killed. Then and only then could I reconcile Jamey's death."

"Oh, Marc," she whispered.

"I know. I guess it sounds crazy but I felt it to be the answer at the time. My parents were devastated but I couldn't see past my own pain. I went through my training and kept asking to go to Afghanistan. After sufficient training, they sent me and I was glad to go. When we landed there, I had never seen such a desolate, barren land. It broke my heart to think of Jamey dying in such a place. I hated it there but I volunteered for every operation my superiors would allow. Every morning when I awoke, I wondered if this would be the day that I would die, too. I went to Afghanistan thinking that I would die."

"Days passed, then weeks, and before I knew it, months were clicking off. When I had been there almost a year, it was time to rotate back to the States. I came home and stayed two weeks; most of it was spent sleeping. Then I went back to the Middle East. I was sent to a different part of Afghanistan this time. That place was just as bad as my first tour. Burning hot, sandy, and poor doesn't even touch the description of that place. I was sure this time, that I wouldn't make it back to America. I took every crazy chance I could but I still came home without a scratch. I couldn't believe that I had spent almost two years there and came home with all my limbs and both eyes.

"I came home and realization hit me in the face. I had failed. I failed Jamey and I failed myself," he declared.

"No, you didn't Marc! How can you say that? Who else would do what you did? You finished what Jamey started. I think you are a hero," she exclaimed.

"No, Callie. I'm not a hero. I love this country but I didn't go to Afghanistan to serve, I went there to die. While I was there, I got some promotions and was awarded some medals. It meant nothing to me. I was supposed to die the way Jamey did, but it didn't happen. I failed at all of it."

"When I got home," he continued, "I looked at my closet full of two and three piece suits and I felt sick. I had let my little brother go into a situation that took his life. I intended to follow him in death, but it didn't happen," he trailed off.

"Marc, you couldn't prevent Jamey's death. It sounds like he was his own man. Just as you are your own man. You have so much to offer. You are a very smart man. In your capacity as an attorney, you can help so many people." Callie searched for words that might ease his pain.

"I came home from the Middle East six months ago. I tried going back to my old life. I even went back to the law firm. It lasted six weeks. One Friday afternoon, I came home from work, loaded my car and left. I drove around Ohio. I ventured into Indiana, then back to Ohio and came north. I took side roads mostly, for no apparent reason. When your little town came into view, I decided to look around and see if I could find a place to camp. Some place solitary so I could be alone and try to make sense of my life. I spotted your woods and it looked inviting. I hoped I could stay there unnoticed," he gave a small chuckle.

"You didn't figure on having nosy neighbors, did you?" she chuckled.

"I'm glad, so glad, that your dad came to see what was going on in his nearby woods. He's been a great help to me. He'll never know how much I appreciate his friendship and conversation. Of course, I never shared any of this with him. I guess I wasn't ready, or maybe I was afraid he wouldn't understand," he admitted.

"Dad might not understand but he would sure give a man space to have his own thoughts and reasons for his actions. I'm sorry for all you've been through, Marc, but I believe you are going to be all right. You have too much going for you to not survive. Things are looking up for you. You seem happy. You work, you talk, you laugh, you even cook, at times," she teased.

"Yes, you're right," he laughed, then sobered. "Callie, I'm slowly coming to grips with Jamey's death. I'll always miss him, just like you miss Dirk, but I'm coming to realize that I'm not responsible for his decisions." He plainly was measuring his words.

"No, you're not. Sad as it is, Jamey died doing what he'd always wanted to do, and that was serving as a Marine. He died a hero." She hesitated her next words. "Marc, he would be so proud of you."

"Do you think so?" he asked seriously.

"I sure do."

"You know, Callie, since I have been here, I've laid many thoughts, troubles, and I guess, fears, to rest. I've a long way to go, though. I've watched you and your dad these months that I've been here. Outside of my mom and dad, no one has ever been so nice to me. I've never seen such contentment and genuine happiness encompass two people in my life. You lost your brother, then your mom at a very young age, but I don't see any anger or resentment at all in you. How do you do that?" he asked.

"Oh, Marc," she lamented, "if you had seen me back then, you wouldn't say that. When Dirk died, we all cried for weeks. Two years later when my mom died with that horrible cancer, my entire world crashed. I tried to be strong for my dad and he tried to be strong for me and we both failed miserably."

"Poor kid. I don't know how you got through it," he sympathized.

"We got through it with God's help, that's how," she replied with confidence.

Out of the Darkness

"I don't have that connection to God."

"You can have, if you want it," she said kindly.

"I don't know, Callie, I'm having a hard time believing that knowing God is so easy."

"Easy? Are you kidding? It is easy for us. We just have to accept Jesus Christ as our Savior. But, let me tell you what it cost God. He sent His only Son to this world to die for all the Callie Hinsons and all the Marc Reeds that would ever be born. What is our part in this? We come to Jesus with a contrite heart and ask Him to forgive our sins and save us. We put our faith and trust in Him. That is what salvation is," she declared.

"Now, Callie, I have a hard time considering you a sinner."

"I'm sorry to dislodge my halo, but we are all born sinners. In the Bible it says, *'All have sinned and come short of the glory of God,'* Romans 3:23," she quoted.

"But how...when did you know?" he fumbled for the right words.

"For me, it happened a few months before Dirk got sick. I'd listen to our pastor at church, He'd preach on salvation and heaven, but he also preached on hell. I would listen and wonder how I could get to heaven. Then I began to wonder how I could approach God. I didn't want to go to hell, that was for sure, but there was something else. I felt guilty, or unworthy, and I was scared to talk to God. One day, it was worrying me so bad, I went to my mother and told her how I was feeling. Her Bible is still on the table by the sofa. She took that Bible and read me some Scriptures, starting with Romans 10:9 and 10. She explained that salvation is an act of faith. Believe on the Lord by faith. Trust Him by faith," she explained.

"I guess I've always had a little trouble with this faith thing."

"Well, maybe I didn't explain it to you very good. Maybe you should talk to my dad."

"No, I think you explained it very well. Now, I need to learn to cope with this heavy load that you just handed me," he teased.

"I'm sorry. I didn't mean to add to your troubles," she apologized.

"Don't be sorry, Callie. You've been a big help to me."

"How?" she questioned. "I haven't done anything."

"Yes, you have. You've listened without judging. I appreciate that very much."

"It's not my place to judge, Marc. Besides, I can understand your hurt and disappointment. Life is not always fair."

"Yeah, sometimes it can be rough," he agreed quietly.

"You're coming out of this, Marc," she smiled. "I can tell."

"Yes, I am. One part of it, that is."

"I'm going to pray that everything falls in place for you. I'll help if I can and so will my dad."

"I appreciate that. Speaking of your dad, I better get you back home. He's going to be worried that I've kidnapped you," he laughed.

"It would serve him right to be worried, after the way he ducked out on you," she declared sternly. "Then he hijacked you into taking me to lunch."

"I wouldn't mind repeating today," he laughed, "with no hijacking, as you call it, involved."

"Well, don't underestimate my dad. He's a sweetheart, but he has a strong will."

They took their empty sandwich wrappers and cups to the wire trashcan and went to his SUV.

Before he started the motor, he turned to Callie. "I have another confession to make."

She looked back at him questioningly. "Okay."

"My name. My name is not Marc Reed. Well, sort of. My name is Marcus Reed Grant."

"So that's why I couldn't find you on the internet!" she grinned.

"I knew you'd try that! I thought, for sure, you'd figure me out," he laughed.

Out of the Darkness

"Well, I didn't."

"Callie, I'm going to leave it up to you on how much or how little you tell your dad."

"No. This is not my story to tell. Your story is safe with me, I promise."

With her answer, he nodded her way and put the vehicle in gear. Their ride back to the farm was filled with comfortable conversation. He dropped her off at the house and drove on to the barn. When Callie entered the house, she found her dad being true to his word. He was sound asleep in his recliner with the tv on and his empty plate on the table beside him.

Not wanting to disturb her dad, she changed from her church clothes, then stretched out on the sofa, as she tried to digest the long story Marc had entrusted her with. She felt for him and what he'd been through. He had tried to run away from his grief and pain but it was plain he'd not been successful.

Callie knew she couldn't change what had happened to him in the last few years but she promised herself to pray for him often in the hopes of one day introducing him to the One that could ease his pain and give hope.

Chapter 12

When Marc joined them for breakfast the next morning he had a different countenance. He acted totally at ease and sported a carefree, relaxed attitude.

Callie wondered if it was because he'd shared his burden with her yesterday or was it because she'd spent half of her night talking to the Lord about him.

She caught her dad casting a confused glance at Marc a few times. She understood his confusion. Marc seemed happier than he had in the weeks and months that he'd been on their farm. When Callie declined Marc's help with the dishes, the two men went out the door to put in another fourteen hour day.

Callie was glad she had the day to herself. After yesterday's revelations, she had a lot on her mind, mostly questions. It was evident Marc had a privileged childhood. Why was he working from daylight until dark helping her dad get his crops in? Why was he living in a makeshift bedroom in the corner of a barn that he shared with Lizzie the cow and her rambunctious baby bull calf? None of it made sense.

With her day away from the salon, she made good use of her time. She planned her breakfast meals for the week, then made a trip to the supermarket to get the things needed for her menu.

The days were getting much cooler so she decided chili would be a fitting dish for their dinner. The rest of the week, Hannah's Diner would be supplying their night time meal. While the chili simmered on the stove, Callie thought of the coming days. Next week was Thanksgiving. Should she cook at home, or order from the supermarket deli? Of course, they could go in town and eat at Hannah's. Hannah and her crew always cooked a large Thanksgiving meal and many of the townspeople depended on her for their holiday feast. She'd ask her dad his preference.

When the men came in from the fields, looking tired, haggard, and dirty, the table was set with steaming bowls of chili. The hard day's work had taken a toll on Marc, but his demeanor was unchanged. He was still relaxed and the serious scowl was gone.

With the meal over, Tom Hinson pushed back his chair and headed for his shower, but Marc was not so quick to leave.

"Uh, Callie. I want to thank you for yesterday. I didn't realize how much I needed to talk to someone. I'm sorry you had to be the sounding board," he smiled, "but I'm glad it was you."

"Well, in that case, I'm glad, too," she responded, then paused. "Marc, I want to give you something, but it's up to you if you take it or not." She reached behind her and picked up a black book from the counter.

"This is Dirk's Bible. I would like to give it to you. I've marked some places that are easy to understand. These scriptures also explain how Jesus loves us enough to die for us. Of course, you don't have to take it." She gave him the option.

He reached and took the Bible from her, turning it over slowly in his hands. "I do want it, Callie, and I thank you, but are you sure you want to give this away?" he stressed. "I mean, it was your brother's."

"Yes, I'm sure. Dirk would be the first one to give it to you," she assured him.

"Thank you. And Callie...." he paused. "Jamey would think you are wonderful."

"Why, thank you Marc! That's quite a compliment. I know how hard this is for you, and I want you to know," she declared quietly, "I sure wish I had known that young man."

"Yeah, me too," he agreed. "We have our memories of them, right?"

"Yes, we do. Now go get some rest," she directed.

He grinned his reply tiredly, "Good chili, Callie. Thank you."

"It's the least I can do. Now, good night. You're nearly out on your feet."

"Night, Callie," he replied and closed the door behind him.

She cleared the table and tidied the kitchen, all the while praying that Dirk's Bible would do its work and Marc's heart would be soft enough for the Word to help him.

Thanksgiving plans would have to wait because she found her dad already enjoying a deep sleep in his recliner.

****

Callie opened her shop Tuesday morning and braced herself for the questions she knew would be coming. Since Marc had accompanied them to church on Sunday, she knew people would be jumping to conclusions. She had to lay those ideas to rest. Marc had given her permission to tell his story if she desired. Of course, she would never tell his private thoughts but his military service should not be a secret. When the questions start coming, she would be ready.

Just as she suspected, she had to answer questions several times that day and the days that followed. She had simply told everyone that Marc had been serving as a Marine in the Middle East and needed some R and R before he settled back into his job as an attorney. Surprisingly, everyone seemed to accept her explanation and the ladies soon moved on to other subjects. By the end of the week, no one mentioned the new field hand at Tom Hinson's farm.

Callie finally got a chance to talk to her dad about Thanksgiving and was touched deeply by his response. "Dad, what do you want to do about Thanksgiving? Do you want me to cook here at home or buy it from Hannah? Of course, I could get it from the deli at the supermarket," she counted off the options.

"Callie, do you remember how our house used to smell when your mom would cook Thanksgiving dinner? I miss that. I miss her," he added.

"She could take leftovers and turn them into a gourmet meal. Everything she cooked was delicious. You're getting more like her everyday."

Deeply touched, Callie not only watched his response to her question, but she listened as well. His little speech helped her make up her mind. Early the next morning, Callie stopped at Hannah's Diner and ordered desserts for her holiday meal. The turkey and the vegetables, she could take care of, but the desserts would take more time than she had to give.

After work, Callie stopped at the supermarket to choose her turkey and all the fixings for her meal. She knew what her dad liked but Marc, she wasn't sure. Of course, he may be going home for Thanksgiving. She and her dad would miss him when he left, but he had parents that loved him and, by rights, he needed to be with them.

Marc attended church with the Hinsons for the second time. After church, Callie didn't give her dad a chance to pawn her off on Marc. Instead, she invited him to join them for lunch at the farm. "Marc, I have barbecue chicken warming in the oven. Do you want to join us?"

"I could be persuaded," he accepted happily. "What can I get to add to lunch?"

"Nothing. It's all covered," she answered. "Just bring your appetite."

At the house, Callie's dad waited in the living room and looked over the Sunday newspaper, just like always. Marc followed Callie into the kitchen and proceeded to set the table without being asked.

"Marc, you don't have to help me. Why don't you take advantage of the time off and rest?"

"No problem. I don't mind helping."

"Did you help your mom in the kitchen?"

"I sure did and so did my dad. Dad always said if we help her out, maybe we'll be able to keep her around longer," he laughed.

Callie pondered his statement. "He sounds like a wise man."

"That's true. My dad is a pretty wise man, and he loves my mother," he added fondly.

"You miss them, don't you?"

"Yes, I do."

"Marc, why don't you go see them? I'm sure they miss you."

"I don't think I'm ready to leave here yet."

"Okay. I'm not trying to make you leave," Callie stressed. "I just thought...with Thanksgiving coming in four days. I'm sorry, Marc, I didn't mean to get in your business."

"No problem. Callie. I'm just not ready yet, but I'm working on it."

"Well, if you're going to be here during Thanksgiving, why don't you spend it with us?" She laughed, "I'm cooking, so be warned."

"I would love to join you for Thanksgiving. And...I'm not scared of your cooking. I find you to be a very good cook."

"We can't go that far," she quipped.

"I'll take a chance."

"I haven't cooked Thanksgiving dinner very many times since my mother died. The first few years, I was too young so we ate at Hannahs. As I got older, I combed through mom's recipes and cooked the dinner a few times, but it was just too sad. I mean, just the two of us and mom and Dirk's empty chair. That's not a good combination. Most of the time we just ignore the holiday and wait for it to pass. This year you'll be eating with us. I think that will perk us up a little."

"I hope so. I understand what you're saying. It was the same with my family. Jamey's empty chair was just too hard to get over. We would either go somewhere for Thanksgiving dinner or we would have so many people over that the noise would drown out the silence of Jamey's absence," he mentioned his own memories.

Nodding her understanding, Callie called her dad and the three of them sat down to enjoy the food she had prepared.

After lunch, Tom Hinson headed for his coveted chair for a nap, but Marc helped her clear the table and load the dishwasher.

"Is there anything I can do to help with your Thanksgiving dinner?"

Out of the Darkness

"No. Not yet. The bird is defrosting in the fridge, the pies are ordered from the diner, and everything else has to wait until Thursday morning. If you ask again on Thursday, I may have a job for you," she joked.

"I'll be over bright and early. You tell me what to do and I'll do it."

"I'll most likely take you up on it. Just don't show off your culinary skills," she threatened. "Because I'm not an expert in the kitchen."

"Yes, you are!" he insisted. "You've made some of the best chili I've ever eaten. The barbecue we had for lunch was superb. You've been whipping up our breakfast for two weeks and its been delicious."

"I know you're lying but thank you for trying," she laughed.

"You don't take compliments very well, do you," he declared bluntly.

"Well, I do when it's deserved," she insisted, "but I know I'm not the best in the kitchen."

"I think you are."

Callie shook her head in mild frustration as she finished wiping the table and the counter. When Marc showed no sign of leaving, Callie wondered what she would do with him for the rest of the afternoon. She knew her dad would be no help because she could hear his even snores coming from the living room.

"Let's go get some ice cream." Marc interrupted her thoughts. "Want to?"

"We have ice cream in the freezer. What kind do you want?"

"The kind you don't have."

"You wanna bet?" she sassed and turned to open the freezer door. "We have chocolate, vanilla, strawberry, butter pecan, and caramel ripple. What's your pleasure?"

"I like rocky road, so let's go," he repeated. "Your dad is asleep; he'll never miss us."

"Okay," she consented. "It's your money."

He laughed and handed her the jacket she had worn to church that morning.

In the car, he asked, "Where can we get ice cream in your fair town?"

"That would be the Dairy Freez. It's open seven days a week. It's little with a walk up window and no inside seating, but they have the best ice cream!"

"The Dairy Freez it is then," he agreed.

He pulled onto the highway and shortly they pulled into the small parking lot "What's your pleasure, Ma'am?"

"Marc, we just had lunch. I don't think I can eat anything."

"Oh, sure you can," he insisted. "I'll get you a small whatever you want."

"Okay. Chocolate. Make sure it's small!"

With a small salute, he left the SUV and went toward the window to order. Within minutes, he was back with two cones in a cardboard tray and a handful of napkins.

"That doesn't look like a small," Callie scolded.

"Oh, come on, Callie, be a sport," he teased.

"Well, thank you for the ice cream, but I'm not sure I can eat all of it."

"I've got faith in you," he laughed.

While they sat and ate, Callie told him about the family that had owned the little ice cream establishment for more than forty years.

"People around here don't leave, do they," he announced, more than asked.

"No," she admitted. "This is home. I know everyone here and they know me. If my dad and I had a problem, people would be standing outside our door to see if they could help."

"I suspect that would go both ways. Am I right?"

"You bet. We all try to help where help is needed. When my mom died, the ladies in town brought dinner to our house for three months. They knew I didn't know much about cooking."

"That was very nice of them."

"What about your hometown, Marc? Do the people take care of each other?"

"No, not really. Mom had a few friends that came around when Jamey died. They brought food, but I don't remember that we ate much of it," he admitted.

"Yes, I know. It was the same when Dirk died, but at least they tried to help. Anyway, I love this town."

"You know, I'm getting fond of this little town myself," he commented. "The people are so friendly."

"Yes, they are. I was born here and I've never wanted to leave."

"I believe I could live here," he seemed to wonder out loud.

"But, you don't. You live in another state," she reminded him.

"Yeah, you're right," he replied, quietly.

They finished their ice cream and returned to the farm. Callie couldn't help but notice that Marc had suddenly lost his jolly demeanor, along with his eagerness for conversation.

When they pulled up at her door, he stayed in his vehicle. With a quiet 'good night', he drove on to the barn. The change in Marc had come when she had reminded him that this little town was not his home. Whether her statement made him mad, sad, or hurt his feelings, she could not help it. It was the truth.

She expected one day soon to find his room in the barn empty and his belongings gone, too. Callie felt very uncomfortable at the thought. She hated to admit that she was sure going to miss him when he went back to his life in Ohio.

Chapter 13

Whatever was causing Marc's silence the night before was evidently gone. He came into the house the next morning, talking and joking with both Callie and her dad.

"You're in a good mood, young man! Could it be because we're finishing getting the crops in today?" Tom Hinson asked.

"Could be, Tom," Marc readily answered. "I want to thank you for allowing me to help you. I have learned so much."

"Well, that's a switch!" Tom Hinson laughed. "Since I'm the winner in this endeavor. I got help that I needed and the gentleman won't let me pay him!" He directed his statement to Marc, then to his daughter.

"Marc, you need to take pay for all this hard work you've done," Callie added to the conversation.

"Nope! I've loved every minute of it. Even those long, long hours were good for me. When I'd lie down on that bed in Tom's office, I'd be out like a light. I hadn't been able to do that in years."

"I'm glad, Son, and I've really appreciated your help."

Callie listened to the back and forth discussion between Marc and her dad. Now that the crops were in, would Marc be leaving them? He had said on Sunday that he planned to be here for Thanksgiving. At least he'd be here to share their day. Holidays were so hard for her and her dad. The presence of a third person would be a tremendous help. She was glad he would at least stay three more days. Then Thanksgiving would be past. The Christmas season was just around the corner, but she'd face that hurdle when it came.

The men left to finish their last long day of harvesting and Callie had a task of her own. Ever since she was a small girl, she'd watched her mother thoroughly clean house before a holiday. She wasn't sure when she had started repeating the tradition, but it had happened. Now, here she was, moving furniture, dusting, and vacuuming every inch of their home as if they were expecting important company. She knew it was actually foolish because she maintained a clean house, but she didn't seem to be able to help herself.

While vegetable soup simmered on the stove, Callie washed her mother's china and set the table in the dining room for Thursday's meal. Her mother's china hadn't been used since her death, but for some reason, Callie really wanted to use it this year. The silver was polished until Callie could see her face reflected back at her. Tess Hinson's crystal was washed and shined until it sparkled.

Callie took her garden shears and went to her mother's flower bed. She cut a variety of colorful mums and some dried ornamental grass and took them back inside. She took her mother's crystal vase and the fall flowers and arranged a centerpiece for her Thanksgiving table. Feeling pleased with the accomplishments of her day, Callie looked over her clean house and was instantly glad she had inherited some of her mother's traditions.

When the men came home, way past dark, their dinner was waiting. After washing up, they tackled their bowls of soup like they hadn't eaten in days. Callie couldn't help but be pleased at the way she'd added to the harvesting by keeping them supplied with hearty food. True, she hadn't cooked all of it, but she had been the one who stopped by Hannah's and picked up their dinner several times each week. She suppressed a smile at her thoughts.

"Now that the crops are in, what do we do tomorrow, Tom?" Marc asked.

"Well, there's maintenance to be done on the machinery. There's always something to be done on the farm."

"Do you need some help?"

"You bet I do," Tom Hinson accepted. "I was counting on it, Marc."

Marc grinned his response. Callie dreaded the day that Marc would leave. Her dad was going to be a very sad man.

While the men continued to sit at the table, Callie cleared the table. She knew the next two days were going to be as full as possible with appointments. Most of her customers would want to come into the salon before their Thanksgiving holiday and Callie was going to do her best to accommodate them. She hung up her tea towel and turned to the men.

"Good night, Guys. I've got two full days ahead of me so I'm turning in."

"Good night, Callie, sleep tight," her dad instructed just as he always did.

"Good night, Callie, thank you for dinner," Marc called to her retreating back.

****

Just as Callie suspected, her next two days were so busy, she ate her lunch time sandwich on her feet. Her shop was lively with everyone expressing their plans for Thanksgiving. Some were going out of town to visit relatives and some were excited about family making their way home for the holiday.

As Callie listened to the pleasant chatter, she had to admit she was actually looking forward to preparing a special dinner the next day. Her plans were made silently and not voiced. How could she explain how she'd always dreaded the holidays but this year she didn't.

If she told that to the ladies, they would automatically jump to the wrong conclusion. Of course, Marc was why she looked forward to tomorrow, but not for the reasons they would think. His easy conversation along with his gift of humor would help keep her mind, along with her dad's, focused on the present instead of on the past.

By the time Callie closed her shop, it was past eight. Her stop at Hannah's Diner made her even later getting home. When she drove into the driveway, strangely, the farmhouse was lit up in the front, as well as, the back. Her car lights fell upon a large, dark luxury car. Baffled, her eyes

Out of the Darkness

strained to see the license plate. As the state of Ohio on the license plate became visible, Callie got a sick feeling in her stomach. Whoever drove that car into their driveway was somehow connected to Marc. Who was it, what did they want, and how did they find him?

Callie dreaded going into her home, but knew that putting it off wouldn't change anything. She looped her purse straps over her shoulder, then scooped up the stack of food containers that held their dinner.

The back door opened and Marc came to meet her. "Callie, my parents are here. I swear I didn't know they were coming. They just got here about ten minutes ago so I didn't have time to warn you. I'm really sorry," he explained. "Here let me carry this for you." He took the containers from her and they walked silently to the door. Just before they went inside, he stopped her.

"Are you okay, Callie? Please say something."

"Uh, yeah, I'm okay. Don't worry. I'm sure they just needed to see you," she said quietly.

"Okay. Let's go in and face the music," he half joked while giving her the side eye.

They stopped in the kitchen long enough to empty their arms before going into the living room to face the unknown.

"Dad, Mom, this is Tom's daughter, Callie. She owns a beauty salon in town and just got off work."

"Callie, these are my parents Dan and Laura Grant. They drove up today from our home in Ohio." Marc introduced everyone and Callie could feel his apprehension. She decided she needed to do whatever she could to ease his situation. Still wearing her coat, she stuck out her hand to the strangers.

"Mr. and Mrs. Grant! How nice to meet you! I hope you had a nice trip. At least the snows haven't arrived yet," she smiled her welcome.

The visitors seemed surprised at her friendly welcome. They recovered quickly and responded. Marc's dad spoke for both of them. "It was a nice trip, Ms. Hinson. Thank you for asking," he responded formally.

"Please, it's Callie. Look, Mr. and Mrs. Grant, we haven't had dinner yet. Won't you join us?" she offered.

"Oh, we couldn't do that. We don't want to impose. We...we just came to find...to see Marc," the lady explained.

"Well, he hasn't had dinner yet, either. Why don't you eat with him?"

Laura Grant looked questioningly at her husband and he just shrugged his shoulders.

"Are you sure, Ms. Hinson? I know you are not prepared for company," the older woman stated.

"Well, no, I wasn't expecting company, but I'm betting I can come up with enough food to satisfy all of us," Callie grinned.

"Uh, could I do anything to help?" Mrs. Grant offered awkwardly.

Callie had a split second to make a decision. Did she want to try to make the situation more acceptable or did she want to leave the awkwardness in place? She opted for the former. "Sure, come on. Let's go to the kitchen and see what we can find to eat."

Callie led the stranger into the brightly lit kitchen and shrugged out of her coat. They both washed their hands and Callie debated on having Mrs. Grant to take a seat but quickly decided against it.

Callie removed a container from the freezer and put it in a saucepan. She handed Mrs. Grant a wooden spoon. "Here you go, Mrs. Grant. You can tend to the chili as it thaws. I'll take care of the soup."

Between keeping a watchful eye on the warming soup, taking sandwich makings from the refrigerator, she set the table cafeteria style. She added crackers and chips as well as the contents of Hannah's containers.

"Mrs. Grant, what would you and your husband want to drink? Coffee, tea, soda, milk?"

"Uh, coffee will be fine."

Callie started the coffee maker and poured glasses of water for everyone.

"Miss Hinson, why are you doing this? We're strangers to you."

Surprised by her frankness, Callie decided to be just as candid. "Mrs. Grant, Marc has been here nearly four months. He's a very nice person, and you are his family. So...why not?"

Mrs. Grant nodded silently and turned back to the stove.

With the table absolutely full of food, Callie called the men to the kitchen.

"Callie, you've set up a smorgasbord."

"Well, it's not fancy, but I bet we don't leave the table hungry," she smiled.

"Miss Hinson, you've gone to way too much trouble for us. We came unannounced. I'm sorry about that," Dan Grant apologized.

"That's perfectly all right, Mr. Grant. Marc's family is welcome here."

Callie knew Marc was trying to catch her eye and she avoided looking at him. If they made eye contact, she was afraid she would lose her composure at the absurdity of the situation. Here was Marc's parents, his dad, the owner of a law firm, eating take out and left overs in a farm kitchen in Michigan.

Tom Hinson bowed his head and prayed his usual prayer regardless of who was seated around him.

"Callie, I'll take a bowl of your good chili. Dad, Callie's chili is delicious. You should try some," Marc suggested.

"I believe I will, Son. I agree it looks and smells delectable." Mr. Grant passed his bowl to Callie.

Callie thought for sure she couldn't eat a bite because of the knot in her stomach but when she tasted the soup, her appetite reminded her she'd only had a sandwich all day.

While Callie was eating, she had time to assess what was transpiring in her home. To say they were blindsided by the arrival of Marc's parent was an understatement. Her impression of Laura Grant was still up in the air. She was a beautiful lady, blonde and looked to be in her sixties. Her clothes, hair and overall appearance was immaculate. Her husband was an older copy of Marc. Where Marc's hair was jet black, Mr. Grant's was more silver. His physique was now giving in to gravity's tug while Marc was still muscular and strong.

While her mind had been going in many directions, she suddenly remembered her role as hostess. "Anyone need anything? Any refills?"

"I'll take another bowl of that good chili, young lady. If you don't mind," Dan Grant handed her his empty bowl.

"Of course," Callie proceeded to wait on her guests.

When it seemed everyone was finished eating, Callie waited for them to leave the kitchen. To her surprise, Mr. Grant was questioning her dad about farming. He seemed amazed that Marc knew so much about the workings of the farm. She was relieved when her dad pushed away from the table.

"Let's go into the living room, Mr. Grant, so we can relax," Tom Hinson invited his guest.

"Of course," Marc's dad responded. "Call me Dan, please."

"Mrs. Grant, why don't you go with them so you can relax. I know you've got to be tired after that long trip today."

"Oh, no, I'll help you with the dishes."

"Mom, I'll help Callie with the dishes," Marc spoke up.

"But, Son, I'll help her," she insisted.

"Mom, please."

"Well, okay. If that's what you want." She relented and left the room behind her husband.

When they were alone, Callie turned to him, "Marc, I can do this. Go visit with your parents."

"No, Callie. I'm going to help. Besides, I want to talk to you. I don't know where to begin. First, I want to apologize for my parents showing up here unannounced. To be honest, I think they thought if I knew they were coming, that I'd be gone. They don't realize how the last four months have helped me. Anyway, I want to thank you for your reaction. You were an absolute trooper. My parents were so surprised, but I wasn't. They have no idea how amazing you are."

"Marc, please, I'm not. When I found out they were here, it was either fight or flight," she laughed. "I chose to fight, not literally," she rushed to say. "But I decided to be as kind to them as I could be and just see what happens. So, now I guess we wait."

"I can tell you, they're impressed. I am, too, Callie."

"You volunteered to help, I believe, so let's get with it, Buddy," she grinned.

He laughed and caught the dish towel that she pitched to him. Side by side they put away the left over food and loaded the dishwasher. Little conversations was exchanged but none was needed.

They joined the small group in the next room and Callie wondered what would come next. It was past ten thirty and their small town was miles from a suitable hotel. As if reading her mind, Mr. Grant spoke to no one in particular.

"Okay, it's getting late. Where is the nearest hotel?"

"Well, Dan, the nearest hotel chain is fifty miles west of here," Tom Hinson answered.

"Look, we have a guest room," Callie offered. "You're welcome to stay here."

"Oh, we couldn't impose anymore than we already have," Mr. Grant declined.

"Hey, my tent is still set up right down the road," Marc offered with a straight face.

With that quip from Marc, the room burst into laughter.

Still laughing, Dan Grant turned to Callie. "How about that room, Miss Hinson. I believe your offer is much more tempting than our sons."

Callie led the way down the hall and opened the door to a part of the house that was hardly used. Mrs. Grant looked around the room and the adjoining bathroom and spoke her surprise. "This is really nice. We're not taking anyone's room are we?"

"Oh, no, Ma'am. No one uses this room. When my mom was alive, my parents built this room with its own bathroom to accommodate evangelists and missionaries that came by the church. Of course when my mom died, that pretty well stopped."

"I'm sorry, dear," Laura Grant expressed her feelings.

Callie gave the instructions that she felt were needed, then headed for the door. She was stopped by Marc's mother.

"Callie, Marc...where?" she hesitated.

Knowing what the woman was asking, she answered proudly. "Mrs. Grant, Marc has never spent one night in this house. When the weather turned cooler, he moved into my dad's office in the front barn."

The older woman colored slightly.

"Good night, Mrs. Grant. If you need anything, my room is at the end of the hall. My dad will be in his room across the hall and Marc will be in his room in the barn," Callie smiled and Laura Grant tried her best to smile back but it seemed forced. Callie wasn't sure if it was a smile or a grimace. Callie was glad that she had been truthful with Marc's mother about everything, whether she believed her or not.

Mr. Grant joined his wife in their quarters and Callie returned to the living room where Marc was seated on the sofa beside her dad.

"Well, they're settled in for the night," she laughed.

Mark turned to his friends and said, "Callie, Tom, I want to apologize to you both."

"Marc, my Callie is my world, and I know your parents feel the same way about you." Tom spoke to the younger man with sincerity. "I'm not sorry they came. I think it was time for you three to be together again."

"Callie?" Marc threw the question her way.

"I agree with my dad, Marc." She answered without hesitation. "Your parents are welcome here."

"Thank you. Thank you both," Marc spoke quietly.

Out of the Darkness

With that said, Marc left for the barn and Callie's dad went to his room. She checked the locks on the doors and turned out the lights. In her own room, Callie wondered if she'd be able to sleep at all, but the long day and the surprise she found at home after work couldn't keep her awake, and she slept.

Chapter 14

At five o'clock the next morning, Callie crept quietly to the kitchen and put the turkey in the oven. She went back to bed and pulled the blanket up close and promptly went back to sleep.

By six o'clock she was back in the kitchen, this time to stay. With the darkness outside and the quietness of the house, Callie was enjoying her alone time. She had just filled her coffee mug when she heard a soft tap on the door. Knowing who was on the other side, she opened the door wearing a smile.

"Won't you come in, Mr. Grant," she teased.

"Yes, Ma'am," he quipped. "I believe I will if you will share some of that coffee."

"Here." She handed him her filled mug and reached into the cabinet for another one.

"Just like I promised, I'm here to help."

"First, we need to prepare breakfast. You want to help with that, too?" she laughed.

"Sure. Especially since my family out numbers yours. I think I'd better help you."

"I'm just teasing. I can cook breakfast," Callie assured him.

"I know you can, but, seriously, I want to help."

"Okay. Can you scramble the eggs and fry the bacon while I make biscuits?"

"Do you know how to make biscuits?" he asked in surprise.

"I do. My mom was teaching me before she got so sick. Then Hannah taught me when I worked for her during the summers when I was in high school."

"I didn't know you worked at Hannah's."

"There's no way you could know. I think my dad allowed me to work there so I would be occupied with supervision," she laughed.

"So you've been a working girl for a long time. Is that right?"

"Yep," she answered and handed him a carton of eggs and a package of bacon.

"You continue to surprise me, Callie Hinson."

"No surprise, no mystery. That's me," she grinned.

They got busy with their separate jobs and within thirty minutes a full breakfast was on the warmer of the stove.

Marc eyed the plate of golden brown biscuits. "If they don't get up soon, I'm going to eat one of those biscuits."

In response, Callie filled one of the hot biscuits with creamy butter. "Do you want honey on it?"

"Oh, man! Yes!"

She handed him the hot biscuit and a napkin and waited for his response.

He bit into the biscuit and his eyes met hers, "Oh, man, Callie this is wonderful!"

"Didn't you make biscuits like that at your campsite?" she teased.

"You know I did," he answered and they both burst out laughing.

"What's going on in here?" Marc's dad spoke from the doorway with his wife directly behind him.

Marc held up his half-eaten biscuit. "This! You've got to try her biscuits. If you liked her chili, you're going to love these babies!"

Callie handed them a plate and directed them to the food on the warmer. She poured their coffee and set it on the table.

Debrah Gish

When Tom Hinson put in his appearance, everyone was already filling their plates. He paused and prayed, then filled his own plate.

"Thank you, Callie, for making your delicious biscuits," her dad commented.

"You're welcome, Dad. Don't forget the honey," she pushed the small jar closer to him.

"Callie, this is a delicious breakfast. Are you sure we're going to be hungry for a huge Thanksgiving meal?" Marc teased.

"You'd better be! Someone has got to help eat that fifteen pound turkey," she exclaimed, laughing. "Besides, we won't eat until about two or three o'clock this afternoon I believe we'll be ready to eat again by that time."

"Will there be any restaurants open around here today?" Marc's dad asked.

"Why would you want to go to a restaurant when we'll have a big dinner right here?" Tom Hinson interjected.

"We just can't impose on you people again," Laura Grant spoke up.

"Mrs. Grant, we're going to have more than enough food for all of us," Callie declared. "We'd love to have you eat with us."

Marc's parents looked at each other questioningly. "In that case, we'll stay for your meal, then we'll be heading home," Dan Grant informed them.

"But, you just got here! Why don't you stay a few days and visit with Marc?" Callie pressed.

"You make a very good argument, young lady," Marc's dad answered her.

"I'm serious. It would be a shame for you to go home so soon. Don't you agree, Marc?" Callie drew him into the conversation.

"Well, sure. Dad, why don't you two stay a while? I'd like that," he added.

"I guess we could stay for a couple days, but we'll go find a hotel. We don't mind the drive," he agreed.

Out of the Darkness

"I'm sorry, Mr. Grant, that you're not satisfied with our accommodations. What can we do to make you more comfortable?" Callie asked.

"My dear, you accommodations are extremely pleasing. I haven't slept so soundly in ages, but we can't take advantage of your generosity."

"If that's what you are worried about, then it's settled. You'll stay here until you have to leave," Callie settled the matter.

"Tom, you have an amazing daughter," Dan Grant directed his remark to the man at the head of the table.

"Well, I could've told you that," he quipped, drawing a laugh from everyone at the table.

When the bread plate was empty, along with the bacon and egg platter, Callie's dad stood up.

"I've got to go check on Lizzie and make sure her boy is still where I put him. The other cows need to be fed, too," he commented to no one in particular.

"May I go with you, Tom?" Dan Grant stood, too.

"Sure. Come on. You'll need a jacket. I have jackets hanging by the door. We'll find one for you," he left the room with Dan Grant close on his heels

"Marc, I can't believe your dad is going out on the farm!" his mother exclaimed.

"Being on the farm will do it to you, Mom," Marc laughed.

"Why don't you go with them, Marc?" Callie asked.

"I promised I'd help you in the kitchen. Have you forgotten?"

"I have forgotten nothing," Callie sassed, "but I can manage the breakfast dishes."

"I'll help her, Marc, if you want to go with the guys," his mother offered.

"Okay, Callie?"

"Of course."

The minute Marc closed the door, Callie began gathering the dishes for the dishwasher. "Mrs. Grant, I've got this if you want to relax in the living room."

"I'd rather help, if you don't mind. I'm not very good at sitting."

"Okay, if you'd rather. I'm going to let these dishes wash while I start preparing the vegetables for dinner."

"Tell me what I can do," Laura Grant waited for instruction.

"Do you want to peel the potatoes?"

"That I can do," the older woman agreed.

Callie handed her a pan, several potatoes, and a knife. She stirred together the ingredients for the cornbread dressing and poured it into a baking dish. The green beans, corn, and sweet potatoes were prepared and set aside to be cooked later. Hannah's yeast rolls were placed in a warm place to rise.

Two more place settings were taken from her mother's china cabinet and carried to the dining room table.

Mrs. Grant had finished with the potatoes and looked around the kitchen. "What else can I do?"

"Oh, I don't know. Anything you see that needs attention, I guess."

"Well, it's your kitchen," Mrs Grant mentioned, offhandedly.

Shocked, Callie jumped and turned to face Marc's mother. "Oh, no, ma'am, this is my mother's kitchen,"

"I'm sorry, honey."

"After twelve years, I still expect to come in this room and see her making something good for us to eat," she paused. "I'm sorry. I shouldn't have said that."

"Callie, I suspect you will always miss her. That's part of loving and grieving," she comforted. "I guess you know about my younger son."

"Yes. Marc told me. I'm so sorry you lost Jamey," Callie answered.

"It was awful...still is actually. One good thing, though, I'm glad Marc found someone to talk to. He wouldn't or couldn't talk to us about

Jamey. He just closed himself off from everyone. When he joined the Marines, I thought we'd lost him, too. When he came back home, nothing had changed with him. He loaded up his vehicle and left. Now, he did call every Saturday but he kept his location from us. Finally, a couple weeks ago, he told us where he was. Dan made some calls and found an address, so, here we are. I just couldn't bear not knowing how he was doing. I visualized him thin, not eating and unkempt, shaggy hair and clothes to match," she laughed softly. "But, surprise! He looks wonderful. He hasn't lost an ounce and he is clean and cared for. I have to thank you, Callie. But, tell me, you and Marc. I mean, is there anything?" she stammered.

"No, ma'am. There's nothing between us. Actually, he's more my dad's friend, than mine. You see, one night this past August, I was coming from work and I saw a light in the woods just down the road. I mentioned it to my dad and the next day he checked it out. That's when he met Marc. My dad visited him everyday. He'd take him food and fresh water. Not that Marc needed it, but my dad was befriending him."

"Marc had lived in our woods at least nine days before I ever laid eyes on him. I came home one day to find my dad in a panic over Lizzie, his favorite cow. She was trying to deliver her calf but nothing was happening. I'm not strong enough to be effective in a situation like that. Dad jumped on his four wheeler and recruited Marc's help. He helped and between them both, Lizzie's little bull calf arrived safe and sound. He had dinner with us that night, reluctantly, I might add. Since then, my dad has found one excuse after another to visit Marc. Dad thinks the world of your son. Marc has joined us here at the farm for cookouts and he even cooked dinner for us one night at his campsite," Callie laughed. "I must say, I was quite impressed with his setup in the woods. He even had a shower rigged up in a tree. I can't even tell you about that. You'd have to see it to believe it."

Mrs. Grant listened closely then couldn't help herself. She laughed until she nearly cried. "I can't believe he's been living this way."

"Actually, he had a pretty good command of everything. He used our washer and dryer, so he stayed clean."

"I'm amazed that he looks so well. I wasn't sure we'd ever see him this happy again," Mrs. Grant admitted.

"He's doing good. He's healthy. He has a great sense of humor. One night when I came home from work, Marc and my dad were in the kitchen preparing your curried chicken. Well, Marc was cooking. My dad is useless in the kitchen," she laughed.

"Curried chicken is a favorite dish," Mrs. Grant confirmed.

"I can see why! It was amazing," Callie proclaimed. "Well, anyway, he insisted on helping dad harvest the crops. They picked the corn and threshed the soybeans. He'd already helped dad and his crew get the hay out of the fields. But, Mrs. Grant, Marc wouldn't let dad pay him. He did a lot, and I mean a lot, of work," Callie stressed. "So, if he wouldn't take any wages, at least we could feed him. When the nights grew colder, dad insisted that Marc move into warmer accommodations. That's why he is in the farm office in the barn, where he has his own shower and bath."

"Callie, I believe you and Mr. Hinson were giving my son something more valuable than money. You were giving him peace and space to settle things within himself."

"To be honest, at first I was very suspicious of him," Callie admitted. "I was worried about my dad. I didn't know who this stranger was. All we knew, he was Marc somebody. We had no idea where he was from and why he was camping in our woods. I was afraid he was, maybe, on the wrong side of the law, or even worse."

At Mrs. Grant's horrified look, Callie had to laugh. "To my dad's credit, he was never in the least bit suspicious of Marc. He trusted your son right from the start, but I was not so quick to accept him at face value. But after a while, I lost my mistrust of him. We've had several talks. I told him about losing my brother, Dirk, who died when he was thirteen with leukemia, then two years later my mom lost her battle with cancer."

"Oh, Callie, I'm so sorry," Mrs. Grant sympathized.

"Well, Marc went to church with us and we were happy about that," Callie continued her story. "After church, Marc and I went to eat and he told me his story. He told me about Jamey and his death. He told me about his own military tours. After his discharge, he said he had to get away and settle things within himself. Now, you know what I know," she announced. Callie had left out so much of what Marc had told her. She felt she would be betraying him if she told all that she knew. Besides, Mrs. Grant would be devastated if she knew that Marc had enlisted in the military, never expecting to come back home.

"I want him to come home, Callie. But, I also want him to come home with a peaceful mind. Do you think he's ready?"

"I have no idea, Mrs. Grant. I don't think anyone can answer that but Marc," Callie answered honestly.

"Callie, are you sure there's nothing between you two? I've noticed he's comfortable with you and you have a good rapport with him."

"Yes, ma'am, we get along well, but this is my home. I live a very simple life. This is not Marc's home. He is an attorney and I am a hairdresser. I don't think that would be very compatible, do you?" Callie lifted her eyebrows.

"I'm not so sure, Callie. All I know is what I see," she replied.

"I guess we better get busy preparing dinner before those men come back and catch us doing nothing," Callie gladly changed the subject.

"You're probably right," Mrs. Grant agreed.

With a final check of the turkey, it was removed and the oven was free to bake other dishes. The two ladies admired the golden brown turkey sitting on the counter.

"Do you want to do the carving, Mrs. Grant?"

"Call me Laura, dear."

"I'm sorry, Mrs. Grant. I can't do that. You are Marc's mother and you deserve my respect."

"Well, okay. Are you sure you want me to carve that beautiful turkey?"

"Sure. You carve and I'll get the rest of the vegetables cooking."

When the turkey was carved and arranged beautifully on the china platter and the vegetables were slowly simmering, both women left to shower and change before finishing the meal.

Callie showered quickly and instead of dressing casually, she was careful with choosing her outfit. She was pretty sure Marc's parents were more accustomed to formal dining than the Hinson household. Callie chose a powder blue skirt and matching light sweater that brought out the blue in her eyes. She applied her normal amount of makeup, not too heavy, just light with a slight blush and a touch of mascara. She arranged her blonde shoulder length hair in a few styles before deciding to sweep it up on her head, leaving a few tendrils loose around her face. After a hint of lip gloss, she lightly spritzed her favorite cologne. One last glance in the mirror and she headed back to the kitchen.

Mrs. Grant was still in her room, so Callie tied one of her mother's frilly aprons around her middle, then checked the simmering vegetables on the stove. The dressing was slid into the oven and the veggies were emptied into bowls. The rolls were tall and puffy, just waiting to go into the oven next.

"I must say, I feel better after that shower," Mrs. Grant announced as she swept into the room. She stopped suddenly and stared at Callie.

"Callie! I noticed last night how pretty you were, and again this morning, but, Honey, you are absolutely beautiful!"

"Oh, no!" Callie laughed in embarrassment. "I could never lay claim to that adjective."

"Well, I think this puzzle is starting to fall into place. I think I'm beginning to understand why my son doesn't want to leave here," she grinned.

"Oh...no...that's not...uh, no," Callie stammered.

"I think I'm right," Laura Grant insisted, then she smiled, "and I don't blame him one bit."

Callie felt her face redden and opened her mouth to deny Mrs. Grant's statement, but she changed her mind and turned back to the stove and the food.

"Don't be embarrassed, Callie," Mrs. Grant laughed, "but I tell you right now, I'm on his side with this."

Callie's eyes widened and she didn't know what to say.

"Oh, Callie, don't pay any attention to what I say. What do I know? I haven't laid eyes on my son in over four months. I don't know what's going on anymore," she admitted.

"You look nice, Mrs. Grant," Callie changed the subject.

Mrs. Grant laughed out loud. "I don't feel very pretty these days."

"Are you ready to cream these potatoes?" Callie held the boiled potatoes in a glass mixing bowl.

"Sure. How do you want me to season them?"

"Why don't you fix them the way your family prefers."

"You sure?"

"Positive."

The kitchen door opened and Callie's dad and their guest walked into the room. "We left Marc at the barn. He's taking a shower and now we're going to do the same. You girls sure have this kitchen smelling wonderful," Tom Hinson declared as he was passing through.

Callie and Laura Grant exchanged glances and smiles and stayed busy with what they were doing. They carried the turkey platter, the dressing, and all the vegetables to the dining room table. The freshly baked rolls were put in a covered basket. Water glasses were filled and a large pitcher of tea, along with the coffee maker were carried to the sideboard in the dining room.

Callie's dad and Mr. Grant had made their way to the living room. The women were checking the table to see if anything had been forgotten. Callie came back to the kitchen for more table napkins when Marc came through the outside door. He saw Callie and let his gaze linger on her face.

"Wow!" he whispered. "Callie, you look beautiful!"

"No, I don't," she answered under her breath.

"Oh, yes, you do. I'm not wrong about these things," he teased.

"Well, you're wrong this time," she sassed. "You're the one that looks good. Khaki's and a sweater? Where do you keep all those clothes?"

"They were hanging in my truck. When I moved to the barn, I moved my clothes in, too. Tom and I built a small closet," he laughed. "You'll have to come and see it sometime. You won't recognize the place."

"I'll take your word for it," Callie quipped.

"Marc," his mother greeted him. "We have the best Thanksgiving dinner! You are going to be so surprised."

"I don't know about that, Mom. I've eaten some wonderful meals in this house," he spoke to his mother but his eyes were on Callie.

"It was a joint effort, Marc. Your mom cooked as much as I did. I think you're going to like those mashed potatoes."

"I think I'm going to like everything. I'm starved! I don't understand it. I can be out on the farm for a few hours and I'm famished."

"I know," Callie laughed. "I think it's the good fresh air. Plus the hard work."

With a thoughtful expression, Laura Grant watched the banter between her son and the beautiful young woman.

"Okay, Guys! Everything is ready," Callie called out to the men in the living room.

The five gathered around the table. Tom Hinson took his place at the head of the table. Callie was on his left and Marc next to her. His parents sat side by side across the table.

Tom Hinson stretched out both hands and Callie clasped it automatically. Marc's dad looked on in surprise but followed his hosts lead and reached for the well-manicured hand of his wife. The hand that held Callie's was beginning to feel familiar to her. They had shared many meals in the four plus months that Marc had been with them and he had always been willing to join hands with the Hinsons.

When the prayer ended, Tom Hinson began passing food. The guests were served first, then Callie turned to the man on her left. "All right, Marc. Now it's every man for himself."

"I like the sound of that, but I insist, it's ladies first."

"Don't say I didn't try," she quipped, filling her plate.

"Here, Marc. You look hungry," she commented, as she forked a large slice of turkey on his plate.

"Is that all I get?" he complained playfully.

"Oh, well. I guess you can have more," she teased, and passed the bowls to him.

When everyone's plates were filled, conversation slowed as attention was given to their food.

"Mrs. Grant, these potatoes are wonderful."

"Thank you, dear. I can say the same thing about the dressing. It's delicious."

"It's my mom's recipe."

"I knew that," her dad joined in. "I'd know my Tessa's dressing anywhere."

Callie reached over and covered his hand. "I know how much you miss her."

"Every day. Every minute of every day," he admitted.

"I'm sorry, Mr. and Mrs. Grant. Holidays are just hard," Callie spoke to their guests.

"We totally understand, Callie. We struggle during the holidays, too," Marc's dad answered.

"I know I'm speaking for my dad, too, but we are so glad that you came. It is an honor to have you share Thanksgiving with us," Callie announced. "And, Marc, we're glad you stumbled into our woods," she laughed. "And, we're glad you are here today, too."

"I'm glad I'm here, too," he responded quietly.

Callie looked away, then back at him. What was going on with him, she wondered. For weeks, even months, he had been friendly in an aloof kind of way. It seemed he was changing. He seemed to be around more and more and used any excuse to linger and talk.

Callie determined this was not going to continue. She would give him no encouragement. With her full time job and her household duties, she knew she had a ready-made excuse not to hang around and talk. She decided she better be using those excuses.

While Callie was having a meeting with herself, the conversation was going on around her. She made an effort to join in on the table talk before anyone suspected her quietness.

When the plates were pushed back, Callie brought the large tray that held Hannah's pies. As each one chose their preference, Callie cut generous slices and placed them on her mother's china dessert dishes.

"Marc, what's your pleasure?" When he hesitated, she laughed. "It's a hard decision, I know."

"I'll take coconut, I think."

"I know what you mean. Hannah's pies are amazing," Callie declared.

Marc grinned and took his pie. Callie cut her own dessert and took her seat again.

When the coffee was ready, Callie started to get up but Marc stopped her.

"I'm closer to the coffee, Callie, let me get it."

Callie sat back in her chair and watched Marc fill the coffee cups. He passed the first cup to her, along with the cream and sugar, then passed the cups to the others. A little surprised, she was having a hard time sizing up his actions.

"How is your coffee, Miss Hinson?"

"Excellent, Mr. Grant. How is yours?"

Marc laughed at her quick wit. "It's wonderful, thanks."

When the dessert dishes were empty, Callie made a suggestion. "Okay, Guys, I expect there's some football games on. How about checking them out while I take care of the table."

"I have a better idea," Marc suggested. "Why don't you and mom go put your feet up and we'll take care of the dishes?"

Callie quickly squelched that idea. "Marc! This is my mother's china!"

"Oops! I'm sorry. Well, what can I do to help?"

Callie stood and began gathering up the dishes, turned and said playfully, "You, Mr. Grant, can stay out of my way while I'm working."

"I guess you got your orders, Son." Dan Grant laughed from across the table.

"I guess I did," Marc laughed, and joined the older men as they headed toward the next room and the recliners.

"Mrs. Grant, why don't you go in there with them and relax, or if you'd rather, you can go to my mom's sitting room that's right behind the dining room. " She pointed to the small windowed room that was visible from where they were standing.

"Nothing doing. I'm going to help you with the clean up," she laughed, "and I promise to be careful with this beautiful china."

Callie winced, "I didn't mean to be ungrateful to Marc for his offer, but..."

"Believe me, Girl, you don't want Marc in charge of your china. He's good about trying to help, but accidents happen. And he's a man," she added with a chuckle.

"My thoughts exactly."

Callie and Mrs. Grant worked side by side, carrying the bowls that were still plenty full, to the kitchen. When the food was taken care of, Callie tackled the stack of dishes that were washed by hand. She washed and Mrs. Grant dried. The china, crystal glasses, and silverware were stored once again in her mother's china cabinet.

"These dishes are beautiful," Mrs. Grant admired the lighted china cabinet full of the dishes they had just washed and dried.

"I think so, too," Callie agreed quietly. "This is the first time we've used them since my mom died. It seemed appropriate somehow. I'm glad you and Mr. Grant came. It made Thanksgiving very special."

"I'm glad, too. I mean, I still feel guilty about barging in on you like this...."

"Oh, no." Callie interrupted. "Please, don't feel that way. It's good that you came. Whether you know it or not, Marc needed to see you. He's missed you."

"Oh, I don't know about that, Callie," Mrs. Grant muttered.

"Yes, he's missed you," Callie assured her. "He mentions you and your husband everyday."

"We have missed him so much," Mrs. Grant confided.

"I'm sure. Maybe things will be different when he comes back home."

"Do you think he'll come back to Ohio?"

"Of course," Callie stated. "That's his home."

"I'm not so sure. I've never seen him so happy and content. He likes it here and he likes the people," her voice trailed off.

Callie felt, also, that Marc liked being around the farm, but this was a temporary stop for him. Soon he would be gone and she and her dad would adjust to life without the man that had become an important part of their lives.

Chapter 15

Callie and Mrs. Grant started to join the men in the living room but at the sound of the football game, Callie stopped. "Do you like football, Mrs. Grant?"

"Forgive me, but no!" she laughed.

"Neither do I! Let's go this way," Callie directed. She led the way to the small sitting room just behind the dining room.

Mrs. Grant looked around at the pale pink walls and the white wicker furniture. "Callie, this room is beautiful! It is so feminine!"

"I know it's dated, but this was my mom's project. I can't bring myself to change it. We repainted it about three years ago but we painted it with the same soft pink that my mom used years ago," Callie explained.

"It's lovely. I wouldn't change a thing." Mrs. Grant turned to Callie. "Tell me about yourself, Callie."

A little surprised, Callie tilted her head in thought. "There's not much to tell. I was born in the hospital in the next county and raised here on the farm, along with my brother, Dirk. I was a typical kid, I suppose. I went to school in our little town, took piano lessons, and gymnastics," she laughed, then sobered. "Things changed for my family when Dirk got sick. I loved him so much. All the modern medicine we had in the world at that time didn't help. He died when I was ten years old. He was only thirteen. He had been gone about eighteen months when my mother got sick. I just knew the doctors would be able to help her, but six months later she was laid to rest beside Dirk. I was twelve by that time. The first year after my mom died, dad and I just existed. I think my dad was worried about me because he encouraged me to do extra activities at school and at church."

"I guess we started to climb out of our grief," she continued, "a little at a time. I entered high school and was cheerleader all four years. I can't believe how busy I was. I also worked on Saturdays and in the summer at Hannah's Diner. Hannah was my mom's friend. She kept an eye on me. I didn't know it then but I know it now," she laughed. "She taught me so many things. She taught me to make biscuits," she grinned. "I finished high school, then went to cosmetology school, graduated, passed my boards, and opened up the shop that I still occupy today. I've never moved out. Dad and I have lived here alone all these years. He would understand if I wanted to move out and get my own place, but I've never wanted to leave."

"I can understand that. This place is so peaceful and quiet. No wonder Marc loves it here," Mrs. Grant commented.

"I have to agree on all accounts."

"Don't you want to know about us?"

"I think Marc told me all I need to know."

"He must have told you a lot," Mrs. Grant stated.

"Well, he told me about his brother dying and his own two military tours."

"Jamey's death was awful," Mrs. Grant said quietly.

"I know. Marc told me."

"Dan and I clung to each other. We were both grieving but we had each other. Poor Marc. He grieved alone. We tried talking to him, but he closed down even more. He went off to the military, came back home after a year, then right back to the Middle East. When he came home after his second tour, we were so in hopes that he'd dealt with losing Jamey, but he was worse than when he'd left," she finished.

"He suffered a lot."

"Callie...,he talked to you voluntarily, didn't he?"

"Of course. I'd never pry into his business."

"Are you sure there's nothing between the two of you?"

"No, there's nothing going on between us," Callie declared. "I promise. I don't know how you could even think it."

"Honey, I know my son. I watched him last night and I've watched him all day. He is tuned in to your every move. There's something else I've noticed, Callie. He would give anything to have some alone time with you."

"Oh, no, Mrs. Grant. That's not true. He's just here to work through some things."

"I'm not wrong, Callie. As I said, I know my son."

"But, that can't be, Mrs. Grant. I mean...we've not dated at all. We went to the next county for burgers once and we went to town for ice cream one time, but that's not dating!"

"Not to you, maybe," Mrs. Grant refuted.

"But, Mrs. Grant, this is not his home. This is only a stopgap for him. One day, and I suspect it will be soon, he'll be gone."

"Callie, I'm going to be honest with you. I don't know what he'd do without you."

"But that can't be so, Mrs. Grant."

Laura Grant sat back in her chair silently. "I just know what I see. I thought you'd see it, too."

"Well, I'm sorry but I don't see any of this that you've spoken of," Callie persisted.

"Okay. I apologize. I'm sorry I misjudged the whole situation," Mrs. Grant conceded. After a pause, she asked quietly, "Forgive me?"

"Of course."

"Tell me about your mom, Callie."

"Oh, my mom!" Callie spoke in wonder. "She was the sweetest person in the world. She loved everyone and everyone loved her. If someone in the church had a problem, my mom was there trying to help. But not just the church, the whole town for that matter. If someone lost a loved one, she was one of the first to arrive at their home with a car load of food.

If there was sickness, my mom would be right there, cooking, cleaning, doing laundry, or anything else that needed to be done."

Callie's demeanor changed and a laugh burst from her. "She ran a tight ship, let me tell you! She was so organized. I always felt like a klutz when I was trying to help her do something," she grew serious. "We loved her so much. We still miss her every day, especially my dad."

"I have news for you, Callie. You are more like her than you think."

"No. I doubt that."

"Look at you, Dear. We turned up here less than twenty-four hours ago. Two perfect strangers, and what did you do? You went to the kitchen and started pulling food from everywhere. Then we sat down to a table full," she finished.

Callie waved her hand as if to brush aside the woman's words. "Mrs. Grant, that was just leftovers and takeout from Hannah's Diner."

"It was delicious. I felt bad because of the imposition we brought upon you but you took it in stride. Then you opened up your home to us."

"Mrs. Grant, this is my dad's home. I'm not the boss around here."

"Who does the cooking around here? Who does the cleaning? Who does the grocery shopping? Who plans the meals?" she questioned.

"Well, I do."

"I rest my case," Mrs. Grant laughed.

"I see what you mean, but this is my dad's house."

"You just run it for him and do all the work," she reminded.

"I give up," Callie surrendered. "But let me go on record saying, it is a labor of love."

"I know it is, Honey. I can see that. Let me say, I admire you for it."

"This is my childhood home and my hometown. I've never wanted to leave either of them. The mothers in this town included me in everything their daughters took part in. This town and the people in it, helped raise me. I can't turn my back on them just because I'm all grown up. So, I work at my business and contribute to the town in every way I can," Callie defended her choices.

"Even if you're alone?"

Callie took the question and mulled it over before answering. "I know what you're saying. Yes, even if I'm alone. But, Mrs. Grant, I'm never really alone. The Lord is with me every second of every day. That's even closer than a husband could be."

Mrs. Grant looked totally confused but she recovered quickly. "I wish I could say that, but I can't," she admitted.

"You can, Mrs. Grant, if you really want to."

"I don't understand, Callie."

"I'm a Christian, Mrs. Grant. When I was a young girl, I asked Jesus Christ into my heart and He saved me. From that moment on, I've never been alone. I lost my brother, it was horrible. Mom, Dad, and I were just starting to adjust to life without Dirk, then my mom got sick. When we lost her my world crashed around me, but the Lord got us through it. No matter how much I hurt, I still had someone to turn to with my pain. My little bedroom has been a witness to so many prayers that I can't count them," she confessed with a sad smile.

"Oh, Callie, I can't imagine."

"Well, it's been nearly thirteen years and dad and I are still on our feet. A little ragged, perhaps, but we're still in the battle," she tried to smile.

"My goodness! What a life you've had."

"I've found out everyone has a story. That just happens to be mine," Callie replied.

"I must say, you've come out on top. I commend you for your strength."

Callie gave a short laugh. "I have no strength within myself, but I have a favorite Bible verse that says everything to me. *I can do all things through Christ which strengtheneth me. Philippians* 4:13."

"And you believe that?"

"With all my heart," Callie stressed.

"What can I do to get that peace, or can I?"

"Put your faith and trust in Christ. That's the only way."

"I'm not understanding," she admitted.

"You know what, Mrs. Grant, I have an idea. Why don't you and your husband stay over the weekend and go to church with us on Sunday?"

"Oh, Honey, we can't do that. This is just Thursday. We can't possibly impose on you until then," she resisted.

"Why not? We'd love to have you stay. You know Marc would love to spend more time with you," Callie hoped her persuasion would be enough.

"I don't really want to leave," she admitted. "I'll talk to Dan and see what he thinks. But if we do stay, I insist that we buy the food."

"Come with me. I want to show you something." Callie led the way to the pantry room off the kitchen. She pointed to the floor to ceiling shelves loaded with food of every sort. Next, she lifted the lid of the extra long freezer.

Mrs. Grant stared open-mouthed at the freezer level full with meat.

"Where did you get all this meat, Callie?"

"Mrs. Grant, this is a farm home. I dare say every farm home around here has the same in their pantry. We raise our own beef. That's why we have every kind of steak imaginable and other cuts of beef, as well. We don't raise hogs anymore but we have a meat provider in town. We buy pork by the case as well as chicken. Now, do you think you need to buy food?" Callie laughed.

"I guess not," she admitted. "Callie, this is amazing, and so smart of you and your dad to be so well prepared."

"This was my mother's idea. She kept a full freezer and plenty of canned food so she would have enough to share."

"She must have been a very smart woman. I've never seen so much food in a home before."

Out of the Darkness

"Well, winters can be rough in Michigan. We've been snowed in for several days at a time. As long as the electricity holds out we're good. If the electricity goes, we have back up with the generators, so we can save the food and still have heat. Speaking of food, I wonder when that trio in the living room will be back in the kitchen for leftovers."

"If I know my men, it will be soon," laughed Mrs. Grant. "Are we going to haul everything out of the refrigerator?"

"No, we won't get everything out. We'll just take their orders and go from there."

"Good idea," Mrs. Grant agreed.

Just as expected, within the next hour, Marc wandered into the kitchen where the two women were seated at the table, waiting.

"Hey, Ladies, would you happen to have some leftovers from that delicious dinner?"

Callie and Mrs. Grant exchanged eye contact and laughed.

"We might, Mr. Grant. What would you like?" Callie responded.

"I believe I could go for a turkey sandwich and a piece of that pecan pie."

"Okay." Callie pushed back from the table.

"I can wait on myself," he gently pushed her back down in her chair.

Callie waved him toward the refrigerator but she didn't stay in her chair. She jumped up and pulled some disposable plates and utensils from the cabinet.

"Here you go, Marc. Use these. Your mom and I are not washing dishes anymore today!"

"Yes, ma'am!" he sassed. "I can follow directions."

The two men, still in the living room, followed the commotion in the kitchen just in time to see Marc carving on a half eaten turkey.

"If your serving, Marc, I'll take a sandwich of that bird," Tom Hinson requested.

"Yes, sir!"

"Might as well make it two sandwiches, Son. I'll take one, too," his dad commended.

"You got it, Dad," he answered while he kept carving.

Callie got up and put a loaf of bread beside Marc and added a jar of mayonnaise. She passed out the paper plates and plastic utensils to each one at the table. She started the coffee maker and put five bottles of water in the middle of the table.

She declined Marc's offer to make her a sandwich and so did his mother. Instead, Callie cut into the pies. She cut Mrs. Grant's choice of pie and one for herself, and Marc's slice of pecan pie. She poured coffee for those who wanted it, but she opted for a bottle of water.

Marc took the chair next to her and reached for her hand when her dad prayed.

"This turkey is even better tonight than it was today," Mr. Grant commented.

"I agree. I always enjoy the leftovers more than the main meal," Tom Hinson chuckled.

"Well, as for me, I'll eat turkey anytime I can get it. My last two Thanksgivings were less than ideal," Marc added.

"I'm sure they were difficult," Callie responded even though he was speaking to no one in particular. "You're home now. There will be many happy Thanksgivings in your future."

"Yeah, I know and I'm very happy about that," he smiled at her.

"We're all happy about that, Marc. Here's your pie you asked for." Callie slid the dish in front of him.

"Thank you, dear lady," he joked.

"You're welcome, kind sir," she teased right back. Suddenly she realized she and Marc had been carrying on their own conversation in front of his parents. She didn't want to give them the wrong idea, especially his mother. This had to stop. "Anyone else want pie?" she asked her dad and Mr. Grant.

Out of the Darkness

"Not for me, Daughter, I think I've had enough," her dad answered and turned to his guest. "You want pie, Dan?"

"No, Tom. I'm stuffed."

"Well, folks, I'm going to check on Lizzie and the rest of the cows," Tom Hinson announced.

"Do you want some company, Tom?" Dan Grant asked.

"Sure. Come with me."

"Is there anything I can help with, Tom?"

"No, Marc. Go ahead and eat your pie. We can take care of it."

When the door closed behind the men, Laura Grant stood. "I'm going to the living room and see if I can find a weather report." She pushed her chair up to the table and left the room.

Callie stood and began stacking the disposable plates for the trash. Marc reached and stilled her hand.

"Sit down, Callie. Let's talk."

She sat back down and waited for him to start talking. When he didn't say anything, she started the conversation.

"Okay, Marc, what do you want to talk about?"

"Callie, I can't even begin to tell you how enjoyable this day has been for me. Not just to me, but also to my parents. You have given us a wonderful day."

"It's not all on me, Marc." she informed him. "Your mom was a big help."

"But it is on you, Callie. We couldn't have had this if it wasn't for you. You welcomed my parents into your home like they were long lost relatives. You gave them accommodations and cooked for them. I don't know another person who would take strangers into their home like you have."

"But, Marc, they're your family. I wanted you to spend some time together. I didn't want them to stay fifty miles away in a hotel. I'm glad they agreed to stay here."

"So you did this for me?" he asked. "Did I hear you right?"

"Well, yes, partly," she admitted. "But I did it for them, too, Marc. I like your parents, especially your mother."

"They like you, too. And so do I. I like you, Callie Hinson....a lot." He took her left hand that was resting on the table top and held it. "You are quite a lady. You're kind, smart, and beautiful. Boy, Kent Phillips sure messed up when he let you get away."

Callie was at a loss as to how to answer Marc's comments until he mentioned her old friend.

"Marc!" She exclaimed loudly. "You dog!"

Marc's laughter nearly drowned out her reprimand. She tried to act angry but her anger was quickly overcome with humor. She joined in his laughter.

"One day I'm going to give you a dose of your own medicine."

"Man, I guess I better stop teasing you about your old boyfriend or..."

"I told you he was not my boyfriend!" she interrupted.

"I've seen your teenage pictures. You were beautiful then and you still are. He might not have been your boyfriend, but I guarantee you were his girlfriend."

"And, how do you know that?" she demanded.

"Because the man would be a fool not to fall for you."

Callie quickly looked at him, opened her mouth to say something. Then promptly closed it, because she didn't know how to answer him.

"Come on, Callie, say something."

"Do you want more pie?" she asked innocently.

He stared at her with that grin ready to break out at anytime. "No, I've had enough. Thank you." The back door opened and she heard their dads come into the mud room. The men stopped to remove their boots and Callie used the time to stand and finish clearing the table. Without a word, Marc helped her put the food stuffs back into the refrigerator and the disposables in the trash.

Their fathers came into the kitchen but didn't stop. They said their good nights and went down the hall to their bedrooms.

"I'm going to bed, too. Good night, Marc," Callie muttered.

"Callie? Are you okay?"

"Sure, I'm fine. Are you?" she asked wide eyed.

"I'm doing absolutely wonderful."

"I'm glad. Goodnight." She turned toward the door, then turned back. "I forgot to tell you. I invited your parents to stay over the weekend and go to church with us on Sunday. I hope that's okay with you."

"Really?" he asked in surprise. "Of course, it's okay with me. I'm very grateful to you, Callie. Thank you!"

"You're welcome," she whispered, then went down the hall to her bedroom. Callie found the living room empty and she knew Mrs. Grant had disappeared to give herself and Marc some time alone.

As Callie lay in bed, she didn't understand what was going on with Marc. Mrs. Grant said Marc was in tune to her every move, and she was beginning to believe it. She was going to have to double down on guarding her heart. One day soon, Marc would be gone and she definitely didn't want him to take her heart with him. Could Mrs. Grant be right in her assessment of their relationship? Or was it just a way for Marc to pass time until he went back to Ohio?

She tossed and turned, pounded her pillow, trying to get some answers. Just when she had resigned herself to being awake all night, she slept.

Chapter 16

On Friday morning, Callie was awake early but didn't hurry to the kitchen. She dressed and took her quiet time to have her devotions. She was anxious to open her Bible and read some of her favorite passages. With Marc's recent actions, she felt the need for direction. He could be pretty persuasive with his attention and his kindness and she didn't want him to get in the way of her judgment. She knew her place and her place was here on the farm. She felt no desire to leave and go anywhere else, definitely not Ohio. She shook off her thoughts. Why get so upset and confused? Marc had not even hinted that she go anywhere else. She closed her Bible and laid it aside. If only she could lay her thoughts aside as easily.

Before Callie got to the kitchen, she smelled the delicious aroma of coffee and wondered who had ventured into the kitchen at such an early hour. She thought maybe Mrs. Grant was up but didn't expect to see her dad at the table and Marc sitting across from him. Whatever they were talking about was not for her because they went silent as soon as she entered the room.

"Good morning, guys," she announced and headed for the coffee maker.

"Let me get that for you, Callie." Marc stepped in front of her and filled her cup. He handed it to her and she headed for the cream and sweetener.

She leaned against the counter instead of joining them at the table.

"Why don't I cook breakfast, Callie?" Marc suggested.

"You don't have to do that. I can manage."

"You're not going to cook breakfast all by yourself and mom's not up yet. So, I'll help," he insisted.

Callie shrugged her shoulders and reached into the refrigerator and brought out a bowl of eggs.

"Here. Knock yourself out," she grinned and turned to cut the sausage roll into patties.

With the sausage sizzling and Marc tending the eggs, Callie stirred the ingredients together for pancakes.

Just as the last pancake was added to the large stack, Mr. and Mrs. Grant came in the room with Marc's mother gushing apologies. "Oh, Callie, I'm so sorry. I should be in here helping you! I can't believe how soundly I slept. I don't think I've ever rested so well."

"It was the turkey," Callie informed her. "Turkey has tryptophan which helps produce melatonin, which produces sleep."

"Really? I didn't know that!"

"And don't worry about it, Mrs. Grant. I had some very capable help," she pointed to Marc.

"Well, he does know his way around a kitchen. All four of us used to get in the kitchen and cook together." Mrs. Grant recalled fondly. "It was a complete madhouse."

"If I remember right," Mr. Grant put in, "you did the bacon and sausage, Marc did the eggs, Jamey did the toast, and he always burned it," he laughed.

"What did you make, Dad?" Marc grinned.

"You know what I did! I had the hardest job of all. I made the coffee, poured the milk and orange juice. I also had to get out the butter and jelly," he stated seriously, but a smile playing around his lips told another story.

The other four people in the room exchanged looks of bewilderment that gave way to laughter.

"Okay, everybody, breakfast is ready," Callie announced. "Get your plate and take what you want from the warmer."

They filled their plates and were seated around the table. Tom Hinson prayed and conversation slowed while they ate. Marc stabbed a wedge of pancake and looked at it closely "Callie, this is the best pancake I've ever tasted. What did you do to it?"

"Oh, just a little Hinson touch," she teased.

"Come on, spill it."

"Okay. There's a handful of oats in there and a small amount of caramel topping, plus a couple tablespoons of melted butter."

"Really?" He ate the last piece of pancake from his plate and got up for more. "Anyone else want more of these delicious pancakes?"

Callie had to laugh as everyone but her held their plates out for more pancakes.

When the plates were empty, Callie stood and carried her dishes to the sink Marc followed her lead.

"I'll do the dishes, Callie."

"No, I'll do the dishes, but you can help me."

"Yes, ma'am, I'll be glad to."

Their dads went to check on the cows and Marc's mother spoke up. "I was going to help you, Callie, but if Marc is going to help, I'll go straighten our room."

She left and Callie faced the same situation as the night before. She was alone with Marc.

"What's your plans for the day, Callie?"

"I don't have any plans."

"Let's make some. Let's go somewhere," he suggested.

"Marc, don't you know what today is? The day after Thanksgiving is the busiest shopping day of the year!"

Marc shrugged his shoulders. "That doesn't scare me. Does that scare you?" he taunted.

"Okay, kids. I made our bed and straightened our bedroom. Now, I'll help with those dishes," Laura Grant announced as she came back into the kitchen.

"I'm trying to convince Callie to go with me to brave those crowds today."

"Nothing doing. I'm taking her away for the day and you men can take care of yourselves," she stated firmly.

"I'm sorry, Mrs. Grant, I have a lot to do. I can't possibly go anywhere today."

"Nonsense. Marc, would you get all those leftovers out for your dad and Mr. Hinson when they get hungry?"

"Of course."

"I'm taking Callie out today. She works too hard. She's always doing for others but not today," Mrs. Grant declared.

"I think that's a good idea, Mom. About thirty miles from here is a burger place that has the most amazing food. She likes their cheeseburgers," he informed his mother while grinning at Callie.

"Good to know, Marc. Thanks. Now, Callie, kindly dry your hands and go get ready to go shopping," she laughed.

"But..."

"No buts. Now run!" she instructed.

Callie looked to Marc for help but he just smiled.

Callie went to her room and changed to go out. She chose a tan midi corduroy skirt, and a matching vest over a bright plaid shirt. Her makeup was nominal, and she loosely pulled her hair up on each side and secured it with a clip. Brown leather boots completed her outfit. She swung a small leather purse over her shoulder and she was ready.

"Callie! You look so cute!" Mrs. Grant exclaimed.

Callie rolled her eyes and laughed.

"Mom, she looks cute in anything," Marc spoke from the door.

"Marc, you've spent too much time in the woods. It's affected your eyesight, as well as, your judgment," Callie spouted.

"Not so. I'm seeing and thinking more clearly than I have in years."

"Okay, you two. Come on, Callie, let's get going. Don't forget to feed the dads," Mrs. Grant instructed as she and Callie went out the door.

"I won't. You girls have a good time," Marc's voice followed them out the door.

Outside, Mrs. Grant tried to persuade Callie to drive her long luxury car.

"I don't think that would be a good idea," Callie laughed and unlocked her own car door with her remote.

As they drove away from the house, Mrs. Grant asked some questions. "Callie, can you show me where I can get my hair done? I was going to get it done before we left Ohio, but we decided to come north rather on the spur of the moment and I just didn't have time."

"Sure. That's no problem. I know the proprietor of a pretty good place."

When the car slowed and pulled into a small parking lot beside a brick building with *Callie's Salon* painted on the window, Mrs. Grant protested.

"Oh no, Callie! I didn't mean for you to wash my hair! You're still having your holiday!"

"No problem, Mrs. Grant. I will enjoy styling your hair. Your hair is beautiful."

Inside the shop, Mrs. Grant looked around. "Callie, your salon is so charming."

"Thank you, Mrs. Grant. Now let's get to your hair. What do you want to be done?"

"I think I need a slight trim and, of course, I need a shampoo," Mrs. Grant looked into the huge mirror and ran her fingers through her hair.

Callie fastened a pink cape around Mrs. Grant and went to work. She usually didn't talk much while she was cutting hair but her silence didn't phase Mrs. Grant. She talked nonstop.

When Callie laid down her hairdryer and her styling brush, she turned Mrs. Grant to face the mirror. "What do you think, Mrs. Grant?"

"Oh, my dear. It's lovely. You are really good at your craft." She turned her head to look at her hair from different angles.

"Are you sure it's okay? I can change it if you want."

"Oh no, don't change a thing. This will make old Dan take a second look," she laughed.

Callie hid her own laugh by busily sweeping up the blond clippings into her dustpan.

Mrs. Grant reached into her purse and brought out a large bill and laid it on the counter.

"Oh no, you don't!" Callie rejected. "This shampoo and trim are on me. Put your money back in your purse."

"But, Callie, I want to pay. You've done a wonderful job," Mrs. Grant objected.

"No charge. You are my guest."

"Callie, I declare! You are so kind and generous. Those are unusual traits in this day and time."

"Now that the hair is done, where would you like to go?" Callie changed the subject.

"Let's go shopping! I'm not really looking for anything, but let's just go out and look around," she suggested.

"That sounds good to me," Callie agreed and locked the salon door behind them.

Forty minutes later, Callie pulled into a large parking lot that was running over with holiday shoppers. They elbowed their way into the shopping crowd but soon stepped out of the main thoroughfare to decide which way they wanted to go.

They stayed close to the wall and made their way down the row of stores. Mrs. Grant steered them toward a popular brand purse store. While Mrs. Grant searched through rows of beautiful leather purses, Callie browsed on her own. When she saw the price tag on one of the purses, her eyes widened and she jerked her hand away. Immediately, she decided to not even touch this store's merchandise.

"What do you think about this purse, Callie?" Mrs. Grant held up a lovely purse that resembled a small over night bag.

"I think it's beautiful."

"Did you find anything you liked?" Mrs. Grant asked.

"Are you kidding?" Callie laughed. "Did you see the price of these beauties? If I bought one of these purses, I'd have to drive it or live in it."

Mrs. Grant looked stunned. "Oh, I'm sorry, Callie. I didn't mean... you must think me to be thoughtless."

"Forget it, Mrs. Grant. I work for a living. Sure, I live with my dad and he wouldn't dream of charging me rent but I don't spend my money extravagantly. My dad has a successful farm that brings in a good income, but that's my dad's money, not mine. I make my own money and I have the expense of my shop, my car, and I pay for other things when I can sneak it past my dad," she explained.

"Still, I'm sorry," the older woman apologized again.

"Don't worry about it," Callie assured her, then grinned mischievously. "Besides, I could buy one if I wanted. I just choose not to."

"Smart girl." Mrs. Grant smiled and led them from the store without buying anything.

They detoured into a store stocked full of Christmas displays, trees, and decorations. With Christmas being Callie's favorite time of year, she stopped to admire every brightly decorated tree. As she fingered the beautiful ornaments, Mrs. Grant watched, then commented.

"I believe you like Christmas, don't you?"

"Oh, yes ma'am! I've always loved Christmas. When Dirk and I were small, my mom made Christmas so special. When he died, then we lost Mom, Dad and I tried to ignore Christmas. We'd get each other something but that was all. No decorations. No lights, no trees, nothing.

I always decorate my shop for my customers though, and to fit in with the shops on Main Street. About three years ago, I decided to start decorating at home. Not a lot. Just a tiny Christmas tree on the sofa table, and some candles. Dad was okay with it. He just didn't offer to help," she laughed. "I've been doing all the talking. How does your family celebrate Christmas?"

"When the boys were younger, we'd have such a celebration. I'd hide their gifts and the boys would set out to find them. I'd threaten them. I told them if they found their toys, they were going back to the store," she laughed. "Of course, I was lying and they knew it. After Jamey died, it was just too hard. Then Marc was no longer around. Dan and I would usually just go away."

"I totally understand."

"Maybe this year, I may try a little decorating again. I'm hoping Marc will be home by then," she added.

"If he is not home by then, why don't you and Mr. Grant come and spend Christmas with him? Our door is open to you, and you already have a room here," Callie grinned.

"Oh, Callie. I know we shouldn't impose on your good nature, but I am so tempted."

"I'm serious," Callie stressed, "but Marc may be back home in his old room by that time. Christmas is still a month away."

"I...I'm not so sure. What Marc wants isn't in Ohio. It's here. I'm more certain than ever that I'm right about him."

"And I'm sure you are wrong,"Callie joked.

"We'll see," Mrs. Grant commented, then continued to browse the store.

Callie noticed the old fashioned red truck with a lighted tree in the truck bed. She pushed the switch that turned on the lights and played festive Christmas songs.

"I've got to have this! Isn't it adorable! It will look so cute in my mom's bay window," Callie stated as she looked around for the boxed trucks that were on display. She found what she was looking for and took it to the check out. When Mrs. Grant showed up behind her in line, holding a foot tall lighted snowman, Callie had to smile. "It's catching, isn't it, Mrs. Grant!"

"I'm afraid so," she answered. "I couldn't resist it! I haven't bought anything Christmasy in years."

"He's a cute little guy. I think he is going to be very happy in your home," Callie teased.

"I hope he is! I'm going to try to bring Christmas back to the Grant household. We've grieved for so long that it became a way of life. I'll always miss Jamey. He was my baby, but we've got to go on living. Our Jamey is gone, but we still have Marc. We've got to start acting like it."

Callie mulled over Mrs. Grant's latest words as they decided to ditch the crowd and head back to the car. She was happy for the decisions that Mrs. Grant was making but she was certain she was wrong about Marc. Sure, he hung around to help her but that was only because he felt a little guilty about his parents staying in the house and having meals with the Hinson's.

Just as Marc had suggested, she took Mrs. Grant to Bea's Drive-in for lunch. As Mrs. Grant raved about the sandwiches, Callie decided to make dinner easy for everyone. She bought burgers and sides for the three men at home. The drive home was pleasant with Mrs. Grant again doing most of the talking. When the farmhouse came into view, Callie felt the familiar welcoming that happened every time she came home.

****

Marc met them in the driveway and took the sack of food from Callie. "I was hoping you'd bring a bag of burgers," he laughed, then lowered his voice. "Who paid for these?"

"None of your business," she whispered back."

"That tells me all I need to know," he reached for his wallet.

"Nope. They're guests and you're our farmhand," she answered with all the sass she could muster.

Out of the Darkness

"What do you mean, farmhand?" he laughed.

"Well, you are! You keep Lizzie company every night and you help chase down her wayward little boy every time he escapes," she said nonchalantly.

"I guess you got me there," he surrendered, "but we're going to have an accounting soon. Especially of these last few days."

"Shh," she wagged her finger at him and handed him a burger.

The ones in the living room joined them in the kitchen which stopped their conversation. Callie wondered how they had made it at lunch. There were no dirty dishes present and the men were still alive; she had to hide a smile at that thought.

After their fast food dinner, Callie and Mrs. Grant hauled out their purchases. The little red truck looked bright and festive with it's lights twinkling and music playing softly. Standing back to admire it, she knew it would look perfect in her mom's favorite window.

Mrs. Grant unpacked her foot high snowman and plugged him in. The changing colors were beautiful. Mrs. Grant set the little guy in the window on the other side of the door to balance with the blinking red truck. The small holiday touches reminded Callie again how much she loved Christmas and what she had missed for several years.

Later when the house was dark and quiet, Callie lay awake making decisions. She decided tomorrow, she was going to the attic and drag down the Christmas tree that hadn't been used in years. The tote full of ornaments were coming down, too. With that pleasant thought, she slept.

Chapter 17

Sure enough, the next morning Callie cooked breakfast by herself and left it on the warmer. With her coffee mug to keep her company, she went to the living room to start re-arranging furniture to free up the bay window for a Christmas tree. Callie heard the kitchen door open and within seconds Marc was beside her.

"What are you doing, Callie? Wrecking the house?" he laughed as he looked over the chairs in the middle of the floor.

"I'm getting ready to put up a Christmas tree."

"Uh-huh, I see. Do you want some help?"

"I do, but I was too chicken to ask."

"Callie," he paused. "You can ask anything of me and I would try my best to make it happen."

"You better be careful making promises like that. You could get in a heap of trouble," she joked.

"No, I don't think so," he refuted. "Now, where is everything stored?"

"In the attic over the garage."

"Lead the way," he directed and followed her back through the kitchen and into the garage.

Callie pulled the cord that let down the folding ladder. She made a move to climb up the wooden steps but Marc's hand stopped her.

"Callie, don't climb up there! Let me do it."

"Why?" she asked innocently.

"Well, because...because you're a lady. You shouldn't be carrying such heavy loads."

"Now, Marc, you know I'm a farm girl," she laughed. "I'm used to heavy loads."

"I know that," he admitted. "But I don't want you doing heavy farm work," he sighed. At her baffled look, he continued. "I might as well say it. You're the most feminine, beautiful woman I've ever met."

Shocked, Callie stared at him. "What? What did you say?"

"You heard me, and I meant every word of it. Don't dare ask me to recant what I said, because I won't," he spouted.

"Okay, I won't," she managed to say. "But...the tree?" her voice trailed off.

"I'll go up and get your tree."

She nodded silently and stepped aside so he could climb up the ladder. Callie's eyes watched his every move as he scaled the ladder and disappeared inside the attic. Suddenly, she remembered the darkness of the attic and hurried to the light switch on the wall.

"Thank you, Callie! That helps a lot," he yelled from the attic and Callie could hear him laughing.

"You want me to come up?" she yelled back.

"No. I want you to stay right where you are. I found a tote marked 'tree.' Would that be what you want?"

"Yes, that's it."

He slowly descended the ladder and let the tote slide down in front of him. Marc stepped onto the concrete floor with the tote in his arms.

"At your service, ma'am," he grinned.

"Thank you, Marc."

"You want this in the living room?"

"Yes, please," she led the way back through the silent house.

He lifted the lid on the plastic tote to reveal the green branches inside.

"You want me to start taking these out, Callie?"

"Uh, not yet. Come on. You helped me. Now I'm going to help you," she motioned him to follow.

"What are you going to..." he stopped when she handed him a warm plate from the warmer.

"I'm going to give you breakfast," she quipped and pointed toward the food on the stove warmer.

"Wow! This is great! Callie, you make the best breakfast," he teased.

"I agree," she laughed and filled her own plate. "How about we have a good breakfast before we tackle that tree?"

"I'll never refuse your breakfast." He leaned close and whispered, "You're as good a cook as my mom. Shh...it's a secret."

She nodded her agreement and made the silly tic-a-lock sign on her lips.

"Tomorrow I'm making those pancakes you like."

"Oh, man! I won't sleep a wink tonight. I'll be thinking about those pancakes all night," he laughed.

They sat facing each other with their full plates in front of them. Callie decided to pray silently but Marc stretched his hands across the table and took hers.

"I believe you pray."

"Yes," she answered. What she said, she wasn't real sure. Even in her nervousness, she was thrilled at his willingness to join her in prayer.

They were finishing their meal when the sleepers began straggling in for breakfast.

"Fresh coffee is made and breakfast is on the warmer," Callie instructed Marc's parents.

"If you'll excuse me, we have a Christmas tree to put up," Marc informed them, then took off after Callie.

He found her holding up the green branches one by one and sorting them by size. "I guess I really should have bought one of those new trees that just folds up on itself."

"Nah, we got this, Callie. We'll get it together." He took over the assembling of the tree and Callie was happy to let him.

"My mom was the last one to put this tree up," Callie whispered.

"I know," he murmured. He reached and touched her hand.

His gesture encouraged the sadness she was feeling and her eyes filled.

"It's okay," he comforted.

She wiped her eyes and managed a teary smile. "Thank you," she mouthed.

"You bet," he winked.

With the sadness receding, Callie dug deeper into the box.

Marc assembled the tree almost single handedly.

Callie followed Marc's directions but it was mostly all him. Within the hour, in the middle of the floor, stood a seven foot Scotch Pine needing ornaments and lights.

"In the attic?" he asked.

"Yes," she winced. " Sorry."

He laughed at her. "Come on. You've got to direct me."

Happily, she trailed after him and watched him climb the ladder once again.

"Ornaments and lights?" he yelled.

"Yes."

As he climbed down the ladder, he was loaded with the needed green and red totes. "Lights first, if I remember right," he commented.

"You got it." She took the smaller tote from him and followed him back into the house.

Tom Hinson had joined their guests at the table when Marc and Callie filed through the kitchen.

"Marc, is she making you work so early this morning?"

"Oh, Tom, she's an awful slave driver. She doesn't have a sign of a heart," he exaggerated, leaving the trio at the table laughing.

The lights stored in the green tote were in immaculate order. Callie"s mom had placed them in such a way there were no tangles. She lifted one cord and the rest came easy.

"Wow! Did she pack these?"

Callie nodded and handed him one end of the lights. She plugged them in and was rewarded with a sea of bright twinkling lights. Together they wound the lights carefully around the tree and started back again. After a few adjustments, Callie was satisfied with the arrangement and was ready for the ornaments.

They moved the tree in front of the window and began adding ornaments. So many had special meaning attached to them and Callie had to stop and show them to Marc, plus give him a short synopsis of the story they held for her. She was really surprised when he stopped and listened to her nostalgia.

When Callie heard dishes rattling in the kitchen, she laid her ornaments down. "I've got to get in there and do those dishes."

"Wait!" He laid his hand on her arm. "Let mom do the dishes."

"I can't do that," she whispered. "She's a guest."

"You cooked it," he argued. "Honestly, she won't mind."

"Are you sure?"

"Positive. Now tell me about this ornament." He held up a small glass deer with a red bow around his neck.

"That was Dirk's. He got it his last Christmas. Mom bought both of us an ornament every year that pertained to what we were doing that year. Dirk had just killed his first deer. So, he got a deer ornament."

"Do you remember what you got that year?"

"Yep, I sure do. I was busy raising rabbits for my 4-H project." She pointed to a white rabbit with a Christmas scarf around its neck. "I got this one."

"What about you, Marc? Did you and Jamey decorate the tree when you were young?"

"Well, we'd start out decorating it with our mom but she'd soon run us out of the living room and finish decorating it herself," he laughed. "And I can't blame her."

"What did you two do?" she questioned firmly.

"Callie, did you ever try decorating a beautiful Christmas tree with two wild savages playing pitch and catch with the fragile glass ornaments?" he asked with a straight face.

"You didn't!"

"I hate to admit it, but, yes, we did."

"Marc!"

"I don't do that anymore," he laughed. "Look, I haven't thrown or dropped one of your ornaments. Doesn't that redeem me? Just a little?"

"I suppose. I do admit, you've been good help today. You haven't balked one time at my slowness or my nostalgic stories."

"No. I haven't. I've enjoyed it. It's been a long time since I've enjoyed a Thanksgiving the way I've enjoyed this one. Maybe never. And now, I'm getting started on Christmas," he commented.

By lunch time the fully decorated tree stood in front of the window with all its lights glowing.

"It's such a beautiful tree," Callie spoke her thoughts out loud.

"I agree."

"Thank you, Mr, Grant, for your help," Callie teased.

"You are so welcome, Miss Hinson."

Marc carried the empty totes back up the attic ladder to be stored, while Callie vacuumed up the tiny pieces of debris that was scattered on the carpet.

Marc's mother came in the living room and stopped beside Callie. "Your tree is beautiful, Dear."

"Well, I can't take all the credit for it. Marc helped a lot. Actually, he did more than I did. He assembled it," Callie confessed.

"I know. I heard you both in here...working together...laughing together," she cast a sideways look at Callie.

"Well. It's not hard to be in a good mood when you're putting up a Christmas tree."

"Uh-huh," Mrs. Grant laughed. "Are you sure that's all it was?" she teased, then looked around the room. "By the way, where did he go?"

"He left a few minutes ago. He said he needed some things from town, but I'm not sure where he was going."

"Look, Callie, what can I do to help you today? We were gone most of the day yesterday, so I know you have household chores to catch up on."

"Oh, no! You're not going to do housework. You're our guest. I'm sorry that I let you do the dishes this morning."

"I hope you're joking, Callie, because I do my own housework at home. I cook, I wash dishes, I clean my floors just like everyone else. I'm thankful that you allowed me to wash those dishes. It made me feel like I was welcome here," she ventured into an explanation.

"Mrs. Grant, you're so welcome here. I've loved having you with us," she stressed. "You've made this Thanksgiving so pleasant. It's been wonderful."

"Are you sure I've made it special or is it Marc?" she asked softly.

Dumbfounded, Callie bit her lip while her face reddened.

"I don't mean to keep prying, but if there's feelings between you two, I don't want you to lose it."

"There's nothing there. I promise. He's just a good friend," Callie insisted.

"You keep saying that, Honey, but who are you trying to convince? Me or you?"

Out of the Darkness

Callie stayed silent. When she did speak, it was on another subject.

"I think I'm going to get some steaks out of the freezer for dinner. What do you and Mr. Grant prefer?"

"Surprise us," Mrs. Grant quipped.

"Oh, no, you don't," laughed Callie. "You come and go with me." Together they went to the well- stocked pantry room just off the kitchen. Mrs. Grant chose two ribeyes and Callie took two t-bones for herself and her dad.

"Now what about Marc? What's his favorite?"

"I'm betting you already know," Mrs. Grant answered.

Callie hated to admit it, but she did know his favorite. In defeat, she reached over the cuts of beef and picked up a porterhouse.

"Yep! I knew it!" Mrs. Grant laughed. "You got it the first try. Not everyone chooses a porterhouse, but Marc always does."

"I think he likes the added meat," Callie mentioned, not knowing what else to say.

"Yes, he is definitely a meat and potato guy," Mrs. Grant replied as she looked over the huge assortment of canned food on the pantry shelves. She picked up a can and read the label.

"Is something wrong, Mrs. Grant?"

"Oh, no, Dear. I just thought maybe I could make us lunch tomorrow. With your permission of course."

Callie had to laugh. "Mrs. Grant, you don't need my permission for anything."

"Oh, but I do. This is your kitchen. This is your house."

Bewildered, Callie answered, "But it's not."

"Oh, but it is," Mrs. Grant insisted, softly.

Callie looked around the room. She knew every can on every shelf and the contents of the two freezers. She kept count of all the cleaning supplies and even the laundry room was arranged to her liking. So, maybe it was hers. But when did it happen? She'd always considered this was her mother's house, owned by her dad. That thought was still troubling her two hours later when Marc came back carrying two large bags full of colorfully wrapped Christmas gifts.

"Marc! What in the world have you done?"

"Just a few things to make that little tree look happier. I think a tree with no gifts looks so lonely and sad." He answered, half teasing but a little on the serious side.

"What's in there anyway? It looks like you shopped for half the town," Callie tried to look inside the bags.

"Oh, no. Don't you look inside these bags," he laughingly moved them out of her reach and eyesight.

"Marc, that's not fair," she pouted.

"I know," he teased. "Come on and help me put these under the tree."

They emptied both bags and Callie arranged them on the tree skirt.

"Now, Callie, you are free to pinch and shake until your heart's content," he pointed to the pile of gifts.

Eyeing him suspiciously, she picked up the gift nearest her. She turned the gift over and over in her hands. She picked up the next gift and looked it over, too.

"Marc! There's no names on these gifts!" She picked up two more and looked them over. Frowning, she looked at him. "You tricked me! None of these gifts have name tags on them," she burst out laughing.

"That's what you get! I've got a feeling that won't stop you from trying to find out the contents of the gifts though," he laughed.

"I would," she admitted, "but I don't think anyone would appreciate opening a gift that was pinched on, wrinkled, and dog-eared on Christmas morning."

"You could be right. But what if all these gifts are yours?"

Callie's eyes grew large and she looked from him to the pile of gifts, then back to Marc.

"Nah, you're just yanking my chain."

"Maybe not," he said offhandedly.

"Marc, you are awful.".

"I could be, I guess," he agreed with her.

"Well, if you are not going to put names on those gifts, I may as well do something else. You want to help me grill? I have some steaks thawing."

"Be glad to," he accepted. "Or better yet, why don't you let me handle the grill and you do the sides. Mom will probably want to help you. Is that okay with you?"

"Sure, she's a big help. I just hate for her to work when she's our guest."

"Callie, Mom and Dad are not guests. Not really. They're my family and we're all imposing..."

She interrupted him, "You or your parents are not imposing on anyone. You have no idea what it means to me and Dad to have all three of you here!"

"But, I do. I understand more than you'll ever know," he said quietly.

With those words spoken between them, neither added another word.

Callie reached and flipped the switch that powered the lights on the tree. Lost in their own thoughts, they both sat silently watching the twinkling of the colorful lights. No words were exchanged, but, again, none were needed.

Chapter 18

Sunday morning was not typical for Callie. She was up early to cook a nice breakfast before church. The knot in her stomach, she attributed to the excitement she felt about Marc's family coming to church with them today.

Mrs. Grant soon followed Callie to the kitchen and started her preparations for her Sunday lunch. "Callie, will I be in your way if I start our lunch?"

"No, of course not. I'll make breakfast and you do what you need to do about your lunch."

With the bacon and sausage frying, she poured two mugs of coffee and carried one across the kitchen to Marc's mother.

"Coffee?"

"Oh, thank you, dear. How sweet of you," Mrs. Grant smiled.

Callie returned to tending their breakfast. The breakfast meats were moved to a platter and scrambled eggs were started. She stirred together the ingredients for pancakes and fried them on the griddle. Just as Callie finished breakfast, Mrs. Grant slid the huge casserole into the oven. Callie handed Mrs. Grant a plate and made a suggestion. "How about we go ahead and eat. The men can eat when they get ready."

They had just filled their plates and were seated when the kitchen door opened and Marc joined them.

"You could smell the breakfast, couldn't you!" his mother teased.

"Yes, ma'am. I sure could.

Out of the Darkness

Callie stood, handed him a plate and poured his coffee.

"You don't need to wait on me, Callie, I can wait on myself."

"Don't argue. Fill your plate," Callie sassed.

"Yes, ma'am," he answered with mock humility.

He took the chair next to Callie and stuck out his hand. She looked at him questioningly.

"Prayer."

Not knowing what else to do, she took his hand, bowed her head, and prayed. When she finished, she caught his eye and he gave her a nod of approval.

Marc cut into his pancakes and took a bite. "Man, this is good. You remembered, didn't you, Mom!"

"Don't look at me. Callie cooked breakfast. You need to thank her," his mother informed him.

"Okay, I will! Callie, this is my favorite breakfast ever. Pancakes and sausage! It's so good! Thank you!"

"Well, I guess it's your lucky day," she quipped.

"I think it just might be," he laughed at her quick response.

Callie quickly finished her breakfast, stood and carried her plate and mug to the sink.

"Leave those, Callie. I'll take care of the dishes. I know you're going to be rushed getting ready for church. So go. I'll take care of our dads when they decide to put in an appearance."

"Are you sure, Marc?"

"Positive."

"Okay, you're on." She started for the door, then turned back. "Don't rush your mother."

"I won't. I promise," he laughed.

Debrah Gish

She left mother and son at the table, hoping they could have some good visiting time. As for herself, she rushed to her bedroom, made her bed, then jumped in the shower.

While she showered, she thought of her dad. He was enjoying Marc's presence more every day. Now, with Marc's parents visiting, he had become great friends with Marc's dad, also. She wondered how her dad was going to react when they all left. She wondered how she would react, as well. The Grants were very nice and she expected them to leave later on today or tomorrow. Marc had lived here on the farm for four months. He was easy to be around, agreeable on most everything. She expected him to load up and leave just any day. Maybe he would leave with his parents. She hoped not. Taken back by that thought, she reprimanded herself. *Don't you dare entertain such thoughts,* she scolded. *He doesn't belong here and you know you'll never leave. No one could ever be so important to make you leave your home,* she vowed. Tears came and mixed with the water from her shower. *Why was she crying?* She couldn't dare face the reason, or was it she wouldn't?

As she dried, curled, and styled her hair, she was still disturbed by her recent thoughts. Sure, Marc was wonderful in so many ways but he would never settle here. This area had nothing to offer an up and coming attorney and she couldn't leave. This house, this town, and her business was her life, but was that going to be enough? Well, it had to be, she determined.

When Callie was ready for church, she went to the living room to wait for the others. Marc was already there and she debated on staying or making an excuse and dismissing herself. Before she could decide, he saw her.

"Don't you look pretty this morning!"

"Well, that's odd. You didn't say that this morning when I was slaving over a hot stove, cooking your breakfast," she exaggerated.

"Well, I thought it but a guy doesn't usually make flirty remarks while his mother is watching from the sidelines."

Callie had to laugh at his silliness. She looked him over and had to admire how he looked, but kept her opinion to herself.

142

Out of the Darkness

"Just how many suits did you bring with you?" she asked.

"Three. Now that you've seen them all, I'll have to start repeating them or I'm going to have to go to Ohio to get more," he teased.

"I don't mind repeats."

"Good. I hoped you'd say that. Hey, guess what I heard on the radio this morning? It's supposed to snow tomorrow!"

"Really? Oh, I hope so! I love snow!" she admitted.

"Me, too," he agreed. "When it snows, how do you get to work?"

"I usually drive dad's truck. If it's a blizzard, I close."

"If it snows, I'll take you to work."

"But...are you going to still be here?" she ventured to ask.

"Yes, unless you want me to leave. Do you want me to go back to Ohio when my parents leave?"

She had a flippant answer but let it die unsaid. With a slow shake of her head, she knew she was revealing something that she'd been trying to hide.

He openly grinned at her and she managed a smile of her own but now she was afraid she had just placed herself in uncharted water.

Marc's parents came into the room, deep in their own conversation and Callie welcomed the distraction.

"You two look very nice," Callie complimented.

"Thank you, Dear. I must say, I love my new haircut! Thank you for working on me."

"You cut mom's hair?" Marc asked .

"I certainly did."

"It looks very nice."

"She has nice hair," Callie answered.

Just then Tom Hinson came into the room, still tightening his tie. Callie looked around the room and silently decided this was a very well dressed crowd. Mrs. Grant was beautiful in an ivory wool suit that looked like it cost more than Callie's whole wardrobe. The three men were handsome in their suits and ties, especially the younger one. At that thought, she turned her back to the group and picked up her purse and Bible.

"I'll see everyone at church," she announced as she was going out the door. She headed for her car, hoping for a quick getaway, but she underestimated Marc.

"Hey, Callie, wait up!" he easily caught up with her. "What's your hurry?" He glanced at his watch. "We've got lots of time before church starts."

She turned and faced him. As excuses ran through her mind, she knew Marc would be able to tell if she was telling the truth or not. She knew truth was the only thing that he would accept. "I...uh..I thought I needed to get out of there," she admitted.

"Because?"

"I, you know. When you...I needed to clear my head and the only way to do that was to be by myself," she attempted an explanation but it didn't come out right.

"Do you mean what you admitted to a few minutes ago?" he questioned.

"Yes," she whispered.

"Hey, you didn't reveal anything. I baited you into that admission," he laughed shortly. "So, I don't know if you meant it or not."

"Are you sure? I mean..., oh well," she stumbled over her words.

"Come on, ride to church with me," he urged.

"No. You need to go with your parents. You've been away from them for a long time. They miss you."

"I know that, but they know," he replied.

"They know? What is it they know? They need you, Marc."

"Okay, okay," he gave in.

144

He kept taking glances at her face. Callie knew he was trying to read her and she sure hoped he wasn't successful.

They parted and Callie nearly fled to her car. Without looking back, she backed out of the garage and out of the driveway. How the ones she left behind were getting to church, she had no idea. There were several cars, as well as her dad's truck on the farm. They could all come separately or ride together. It didn't matter to her. All she knew was, that she needed to be alone.

To show Dan and Laura Grant that she wasn't entirely without manners, Callie waited in the church parking lot for her group to arrive so they could walk in together. On the way into the church, Marc moved beside her.

"Callie, are you okay?" he asked under his breath.

"Yes," she managed an embarrassed laugh. "I'm sorry, Marc. I acted so stupidly."

"Never. It's good between us, right?"

"Yes, we're good," she returned and entered the church with her dad and their guests.

****

After the service, they enjoyed Mrs. Grant's delicious casserole, a green salad, and Hannah's puffy rolls. The food was wonderful and the conversation was lively. Mrs. Grant was full of questions and she didn't mind asking them. The questions she asked told Callie the depth of her interest. She listened, and so did Marc, as her dad sufficiently answered her Bible questions. Mr. Grant was rather quiet but Callie suspected his wife was asking questions for the both of them. She hoped and prayed that the sermon they had heard this morning, along with her dad's instructions, would go with them when they traveled back to Ohio.

After lunch, Callie insisted that Mrs. Grant go and relax and let her clear the table, but to no avail. The older woman covered the leftovers and put them away while Callie loaded the dishwasher and wiped the table and counter.

"Mrs. Grant, you need to give me that recipe. Marc made that dish one night for dinner, but hedged when I asked him for the recipe."

"Maybe he thought you'd keep him around to cook, if you didn't know the recipe," she laughed.

"Hardly that," Callie refuted. She looked out the window at the sky that was getting gray with familiar looking clouds. "Looks like those snow clouds are starting to roll in."

"Oh, no. Snow! I guess we need to load up and head toward home before it comes," she joined Callie at the window.

"Wouldn't it be exciting to get snowed in here at the farm?" Callie could barely contain her excitement.

"Oh, Honey! I can't think of anything I would like more, but we've got to get home. Dan has obligations at the office," she sighed.

"I understand. But do you have to leave today? Can't you stay one more night?" Callie urged.

"I don't know, but I'll speak to Dan. I love watching him here on the farm. He looks so relaxed and rested."

"Well, I agree that the farm is slow moving and quiet. Unless you have a cow having trouble calving or the combine tears up when you're half finished with your last field," Callie laughed.

Mrs. Grant joined her laughter, then grew serious. "Callie, do you ever see yourself moving away?"

"I...I really don't know. There has never been a cause to present itself where I would want to leave or feel the need to leave."

"What if someone presented himself, would that be reason enough?"

"Well, no one has, so I haven't had to think about that."

"Are you sure about that?" Mrs. Grant questioned.

"Yes, ma'am. I'm positive."

Mrs. Grant looked like she wanted to say something else, but she didn't. She hesitated, then smiled. "I guess I better go give Dan the weather report," she stated, then went toward the living room to find her husband.

Out of the Darkness

Callie didn't want to join the group in her own living room and tried to find a good excuse not to but none came to mind. She finally went to the living room and found the Christmas tree blinking. There was no doubt who had flipped the switch that was on the floor beside the chair occupied by Marc.

Her dad and Marc were seated in the matching recliners and Mr. and Mrs. Grant were side by side on the sofa. Callie took the chair that was farthest from all of them. She sat in her mom's rocking chair where she had full view of the lit tree. Maybe if she pretended to be enthralled by the twinkling lights, no one would expect conversation from her.

Even though she was silent, her mind was running in high gear. She had so many questions and they were mostly about herself. Why was she so miserable? No one was demanding anything of her. Did she want pressure? No, she was pretty sure she didn't. Was it Marc? He had been nothing but nice to her and helpful to her dad. Why did she feel like he knew her thoughts and moods even when she hid them from herself? Besides, he would soon be leaving, she was sure of that. That thought gave her a knot in her stomach. When he did leave, she would probably never see or hear from him again. Things would go back the way they were before she saw the light in the darkness last August. It would be her, her dad, and her job. She had been happy and content but for some reason she felt those days were gone. Her thoughts seemed to stifle her. Maybe she needed some fresh air.

"I think I'm going outside to check out those clouds," she spoke to no one in particular. As she walked across the room, she felt four pairs of eyes following her. That made her want to escape even more. She took her hooded sweatshirt from the rack in the mudroom and headed out the door.

Her mother's bench had an assortment of leaves on the seat. She brushed them away and sat down. She missed her mother so much. She needed her advice on so many fronts. Her dad loved her but she knew he had no advice for her. Callie's mind played a scene with her mother that she had visited time after time. About five days before she died, Tessa Hinson held her daughter and told her she would soon be leaving. Next, her mother opened her Bible to Psalm chapter twenty-seven, verse ten and read it to her. *When my father and my mother forsake me, then the Lord will take me up.* After thirteen years, Callie knew the Lord would take her up but there were times, and this was one of them, that she desperately needed her mom. What was she so upset about? She felt like her happy world was slipping away.

"Could this unhappy girl use some company?"

Callie jumped at Marc's voice. She hadn't heard him approach. Maybe he could help her. But how? That was another one of her questions.

"Sure," was all she could manage.

"What's wrong, Callie?"

"I don't really know, Marc. I just have a sad feeling. I don't understand it."

"What are you sad about? Has my mom hurt your feelings in some way?"

"No..,oh, no! Your mom is a lovely woman. She's very kind to me."

"Why are you sad?" he probed.

"I don't know. I think I'm afraid."

"What are you afraid of?"

"I don't know. It's just a feeling, I guess."

"Callie, be honest with me. Am I causing this problem? Do I need to leave?" he asked quietly.

At the thought of him actually leaving caused her eyes to fill. "No, but I know you're going to," she whispered.

"Do you want me to leave?"

"No," with a shake of her head, the tears left her eyes and ran down her face.

"Why are you crying?"

"I'm not crying," she denied and dabbed quickly at her wet eyes.

"Callie, we need to talk. I mean, seriously talk. For nearly four months now, we've talked, we've bantered back and forth. We've learned a lot about each other. We've seen each other at our best and sometime at our worst," he declared.

"And sometime, we couldn't tell one from the other," she smiled weakly.

"Now, that's true," he admitted. "What I'm trying to say, Callie, is I have feelings. Deep feelings for you," he admitted.

"But, Marc, you're leaving," she whispered, tearing up again.

"Well, I'm here now. Doesn't that count?"

"Yes, for now, but..,"

"No buts. I don't want you to worry about me leaving. I mean, true, I'll have to go at some point and start working again, but I still have a while."

"But how long?" She looked him in the eye.

"That might depend on you. I mean, if we have something between us, I want to give us time to see what we have. If you don't want me, then I'll leave. There's no use in beating a dead horse and making you miserable in the process. So...you tell me. Do we have anything between us?" he questioned.

Callie considered his words. She knew what she wanted to say. She cared...a lot. As much as she wanted, she couldn't say what he wanted to hear. She had prayed for him to come to Christ and receive salvation, but so far it hadn't happened. She couldn't tell him she loved him but she had to tell him she cared.

"I care, Marc. I really do."

"That's all I need to know. If you care for me, I'll move whatever is in the way to make it work," he promised.

"But Marc, your parents miss you. They need you. They have no other family but you."

"I'm aware of that. But, Callie, your dad will miss you, too. He needs you. He, also, has no family but you," he repeated her own words back to her.

"So. Where does that leave us, Marc? It looks like we're back to square one," she said sadly.

"No, not near square one. Of course, there's some things to be worked through. Some decisions to be made, but we'll do what we need to do."

"How are we going to make it work if you're in Ohio and I'm here in Michigan?"

"It will be harder, I admit. But if we have something strong enough, it can stand some distance for a while. Don't you agree?"

"I'd want to think so," she hesitated.

"Do I hear a but?"

"Marc, I'm so glad you came to our little town, especially to our woods, and I'm glad you stayed. I'm glad we became whatever we are," she tried to laugh but failed. "But, you'll soon be going away. I can feel it, and when you go back to your home, I don't think you'll ever be back."

"Callie, that's not true. If and when I go back to Ohio, I'll be back, I promise," he vowed.

"What about your parents?" She just couldn't get past that question.

"My parents? My parents won't keep us apart. They wouldn't even want to."

"Your mom knows, Marc," she uttered.

"What do you mean, 'my mom knows'?" he frowned.

"She told me she thinks there's something between us. She said you would like to have some time alone with me," she glanced at him, embarrassed. Callie didn't know what his answer was going to be but she certainly didn't expect the response she got.

He threw back head and laughed loudly into the cool air.

"My mom knows her son. Callie, I've wanted to talk to you alone for weeks. I've tried to think up reasons to be in the house so I could talk to you. I've wanted to tell you that my friendship was changing into love, but there never was a time or place for it, but my mom is absolutely right," he confirmed.

"I told her she was mistaken but she didn't buy it," Callie tried not to laugh when she thought of the conversations with his mother. Marc caught her eye and they broke into laughter.

"If she asks you now, what are you going to say?" he teased.

Callie thought for a second before she answered. "I'll tell her to talk to her son."

"Go ahead. I'll gladly spill the beans," he countered.

"All joking aside, what are we going to do, Marc?"

"Callie, trust me. I'm trying to figure this out. One thing is for sure, I'm here for the long haul. I don't intend to lose you. Do you believe me?"

"Yes, but.." she started but he interrupted her.

"No buts, remember? I don't want you to feel any pressure. Let me have the pressure. When I figure out a way to make this work, I'll let you know. It won't hurt anything if you pray for me while I'm looking into a few things," he mentioned.

Her eyes widened at his last comment. Maybe her prayers will be answered after all. "I will pray. I promise."

He gave her that look that she loved. The look that was partly teasing with a dose of flirtiness but still retained some seriousness.

"Are you getting cold?" He reached and felt her hands clasped in her lap. He didn't let go.

"Not really. Just my hands."

"I can take care of those hands." He took both her hands in his and held them.

"Do you think we need to go back inside now?"

"I don't want to," he chuckled, "but I guess we should go in and assure them we haven't killed each other."

"What are we going to tell them?"

"Nothing. We're not going to tell them anything. We're going back in there and I'm going to continue to sit beside you and tease you. I may even flirt a little here and there, just like I have been, or haven't you noticed?" he grinned.

"Oh, yes, I've noticed but I thought, maybe, I was imagining things."

"Before we go back inside, Callie, there's something I want to say. I've had girlfriends, mostly in college, but I never really cared for them. I've never loved until now. It seems I have looked for you my whole life. Now that I've found you, I'm going to pursue you with all my might. Is that acceptable to you?"

"Yes, it's perfectly acceptable to me."

He grinned at her, stood and held out his hand. Together, hand in hand, they walked back to the house to face parents that would be trying to figure out what their children had been talking about on Tessa Hinson's garden bench.

At the door, Callie turned back to Marc and whispered, "Are my eyes red from crying?"

"Your eyes are beautiful, red or not," he whispered back.

As they entered the house and the living room, expecting three pairs of eyes to be on them, they were not disappointed.

Chapter 19

The next morning after breakfast, Callie, her dad, and Marc stood shoulder to shoulder, in the skiff of falling snow, saying goodbye to Marc's parents.

"Listen, you folks are welcome here anytime. Your bedroom will be ready. Callie will see to that," Tom Hinson informed the departing couple.

Marc hugged each of his parents and instructed them to drive carefully in the snow. Mrs. Grant said something to Marc which Callie couldn't hear but Marc's "Soon" reached her loud and clear and she knew what that word meant.

Mr. Grant approached Callie and stuck out his hand. With her hand in both of his, he gave her a huge smile. "Callie, thank you for everything. I have never had a more enjoyable holiday and it's mostly because of you," he declared seriously.

"The pleasure was mine, Mr. Grant. I hope you and Mrs. Grant will come again."

"Oh, my dear, I think you can count on that," he smiled.

Mrs. Grant stepped in front of her husband, embraced Callie, and whispered, "Callie, thank you for allowing us to be here and giving us the time to get to know you. My son is so happy and I thank you for that. I hope to come back real soon."

Callie smiled at Mrs. Grant and answered her as honestly as she knew how.

"Thank you for coming. Dad and I loved having you here, especially me. And you were right about Marc and me. Where it's going? I don't know, but I think he's the most wonderful man I have ever met."

"It'll work its way to where it's supposed to be. You'll see," Mrs. Grant stated. She stepped away from Callie and took her hands. "Thank you, Callie for putting up with us and feeding us so well. You're one in a million."

"You are so very welcome. Please come back soon."

"Oh, don't worry. We'll be back," Marc's mother answered and released her hands.

Callie stood between her dad and Marc as they watched the car leave the driveway and head toward town.

"I wish they didn't have to leave. I loved having them here," Callie uttered.

"Thank you, Callie, for being so nice to them."

"You're welcome. They're easy to be nice to."

They went back into the house, Callie to the kitchen and her dad to put on farm clothes. Marc lingered in the kitchen with Callie. The breakfast dishes were stacked in the sink instead of being washed earlier. Callie had wanted to spend as much time as possible with Marc's parents.

"Callie, my parents adore you. They can't believe how you juggled having two unexpected guests thrown at you, on Thanksgiving, no less. You pulled it off with flying colors. You're amazing," he complimented.

"It wasn't hard and besides, your mother helped with everything. I like her."

"I'm glad to hear that. Especially since you'll be seeing her frequently in our future, I hope," he winked at her.

"I'd like that," she grinned, then sobered. "How long are you going to be here, Marc? I heard you tell your mom that you'd see her soon."

"I'd like to stay here until the first of the year. Then, I'll go home and figure out my...our next step. I want to spend Christmas here with you. How does that sound?"

Out of the Darkness

"I'd like that. I used to love Christmas. The last few years, not so much. I'd like to enjoy it once again. Having you here will help me do that," she smiled.

"I think I can help pull that off for you. I'll be here, I promise." He gave her that look that she loved.

"What have you and Dad got planned for today?" Callie asked, changing the subject.

"I don't know. I'll have to ask Tom. First, though, I need to run an errand in town. Do you need anything? From the supermarket or from Hannah's?" he offered.

"No. I don't need anything. Just be careful on the snow," Callie warned.

"I will, Honey. I'll be back in a little while." He nodded at her and smiled as he went out the door and Callie turned back to the sink full of dishes.

Her dad found her there when he stopped by the kitchen.

"I guess you and Marc got things worked out between you?"

"Well, some, I guess. We care for each other very much, but Dad, I can't commit to him, because he's not committed to Christ. You know.."

"Wait! Wait!" He interrupted her. "Callie, Marc didn't want me to tell you, but he gave his heart to Christ more than three weeks ago."

"What? Why didn't he tell me?" she demanded.

"He didn't tell you because he didn't want you to think he accepted Christ just to get in good with you," he reasoned.

"But Dad, I would never think that!"

"Oh, yes, you would. I know you, Callie, and so does Marc. If someone comes to you, they better have their ducks in a row and receipts in hand. Just like your sweet mama," he answered quietly.

"Dad, this changes everything between Marc and me. I've been reluctant to let him know how I really feel."

"Callie-girl, I want you to know, I wish you all the happiness in the world. I couldn't find a better man for you. Marc is a wonderful guy," he finished his thoughts.

"Thank you, Dad," she replied and blinked back her tears.

With his own face flushed with emotion, he nodded Callie's way and went out the door.

Callie finished the dishes, then prepared the beef and vegetables for her dad's favorite stew. While her hands were busy, her mind was even busier. Marc's decision for Christ was a game changer. She no longer had doubts about him. Now her dilemma was leaving her dad and her home. How was she going to do that? Of course, Marc hadn't asked that of her yet. Maybe he won't. He might not have long term plans for them, even though he was talking about them in general. She needed to talk to him soon. She had questions only he could answer them.

Callie finished freshening up the guest room, even though Mrs. Grant had left it spotless. She washed the sheets, blanket, and the comforter. When Callie closed the door behind her, she left the room impeccable and ready for the return of the Grants. Secretly, she hoped they would return for Christmas.

Callie watched for Marc's return. When he arrived back from town, she found it odd that he had no boxes or bags to show for it. He came straight to the house and Callie had the door open for him.

"No bags? You went to town, I believe," she stated.

"Yes, ma'am, I went to town, and, no, I have no bags," he grinned.

She couldn't wait for him to bring up his conversion. After all, he hadn't breathed a word about it in nearly four weeks. So she brought up the subject herself.

"Marc, my dad said you became a Christian a few weeks ago. Is that right?" she asked.

"Yes."

"Why didn't you tell me?"

"I didn't tell you because I didn't want you to think that I became a Christian just to have a chance with you," he explained. "I wanted to keep the two decisions separate. My meeting with Christ had to come first, then I felt I could present my case to you."

"I understand, Marc. I am so happy for you," she hesitated. "And I'm happy for me, too."

The inquisitive look he gave her made her explain further. "Uh, I couldn't make a commitment to you until you became a Christian. Do you understand?"

"I do. Does that mean, now you can commit?" he asked.

"Yes."

"Those words are music to my ears," he grinned. "We're going to be okay, Callie. Together we'll work through every obstacle. Are you willing?"

"Yes, I'm willing."

"You've made me a happy man, Callie. I'm working on something regarding our future. When it's a done deal, I'll tell you all about it. Until then, we'll pray. Okay?" he stated seriously.

"I'm in," she responded.

He reached for her and she willingly stepped into his arms. He held her. No words, no pressure, just comfort.

When he went to the barn, Callie nearly floated through her housework and her preparations for work the next day.

Marc joined them for dinner and the atmosphere was relaxed and cheerful. He kept them entertained with stories of his high school years and his short football career. Many of his stories were so funny that they kept Callie and her dad in side-splitting laughter. Marc had totally lost the quiet, reserved person that he had carried with him when he first came and for months after.

After Tom Hinson had gone to bed, Marc and Callie stayed up and visited. Callie was so thrilled that he was opening up and sharing his past with her, as well as the present. He confided in her about his relationship with his brother and how lost he felt without him. Callie let him know that she could share his sympathy in that regard. True, her brother hadn't been killed on foreign soil, but she figured that loss was loss, no matter how it happened.

When Marc went to his room in the barn, Callie went to bed with a heart full of happiness. She was careful to thank her Lord for saving the man that she loved. She lengthened her prayer to include Marc's parents. Her mind took off in another direction. What would they really think of her and Marc? Would they accept her or would they resent her? After all, he had left all that was familiar to him and wound his way around the country until he ended up in their woods. She knew they wanted him home and happy, but would they want her, too? She prayed about it and felt a measure of contentment in allowing Marc to pave the way for her, if it's meant to be. With that thought, she settled down to sleep.

****

Callie was glad to see her customers. Through the years, many clients had become dear friends. Even though Marc had been regular at church for several weeks and he was often seen around their small town, no one seemed to be putting two and two together and coming up with Marc and Callie as a couple. With no one else saying anything, she certainly wasn't going to enlighten them.

In the past, Callie had always been freely willing to take last minute appointments and work late, but now her eyes frequently watched the clock. She found herself wishing for some cancellations so she could hurry home. The only reason was Marc. Just the thought of him brought a smile to her lips and made her heart beat a little faster.

For several days, Callie kept the same schedule and routine. She made breakfast and left it on the warmer on the stove and she picked up dinner at Hannahs. By Thursday, Callie was looking forward to the weekend. Fridays were always busy so the day would fly by and Saturday's half day would be filled mostly with haircuts. Then she would have some time to spend with Marc.

On Friday, as they were finishing dinner, Marc asked her for a date, right in front of her dad.

"Callie, when you get home from work tomorrow, let's get dressed up and go to a nice restaurant. Want to?"

"Are you asking me for a date?" she pretended innocence.

"I am."

"Well, in that case, the answer is yes," she accepted, then looked at her dad.

"Don't look at me," he declared. "I want you to go with Marc. That means I'll have the night and the remote to myself," he laughed. "You two know I'm teasing, but I do want you to go out, have some fun. Do something other than farm work for a change. I won't even miss you," he teased.

Marc and Callie couldn't help laughing at her dad. He was happy for the young couple at his table and he didn't try to hide it.

On Saturday after work, Callie rushed home and prepared a large chef salad for her dad's dinner. She took her time in getting ready for her date. That word seemed foreign to her. It had been a few years since she'd had a real date and being with Marc made it even more special.

She chose her favorite nice dress. The royal blue brought out the color of her eyes and was a lovely contrast to her blond hair. She waffled between her highest heels or her lower pumps. The height didn't matter because which one she chose, she would still barely reach Marc's shoulder. Choosing the higher heels, she topped her outfit with a soft ivory cape that her dad had bought her last Christmas.

When Marc came in the door, he stopped in his tracks and gave a soft wolf whistle. "You look beautiful."

"Would you stop it," she laughed to cover her embarrassment.

"No. I will not!" he replied. "You are a beautiful woman and I want you to get used to hearing it."

"You don't have to say that, Marc."

"Well, I'm not going to argue about it," he laughed, then grew serious, "but I am very proud to have you as my date."

Callie looked over his navy suited frame and approved. "And I'm very glad to be seen with you," she returned. "No matter where we're going."

"I got online and looked up some restaurants. I found one that boasted the best steaks in three states," he laughed. "So I thought I'd see if their advertising is correct. We have reservations for seven."

"Um, that sounds good! I'm ready when you are," she reached for her cape.

"I believe that's my job," he took the cape from her and wrapped it around her. "I could get used to this," he whispered.

She turned and smiled shyly. "Me, too."

"Are you ready, Miss Hinson?" He offered her his arm.

"I am, sir," she teased back.

"Well, let's go. Our reservations are seventy miles away. I'm going to enter the address in my GPS and let her lead us."

They went to Marc's SUV and Callie searched the yard and barn area for a glimpse of her father. He came around the corner of the barn and gave them a wide arm wave. Callie and Marc waved back and climbed into the vehicle.

"Are you worried about him, Callie?" he seemed to read her mind.

"Yes, I guess I am. It's hard not to. It's just been the two of us all these years," she attempted an explanation.

"I understand, Honey. We'll keep an eye on him together. I've grown to love him, too. He has been so good to me and so helpful," he assured her.

"Thank you, Marc. I don't know how to thank you."

"No problem. After all, you're going to have a relationship with my parents soon. So, I think we're even," he laughed.

Callie enjoyed every minute of the car ride to their destination. The hour long drive seemed to fly by, making her wish the trip could've been longer. The restaurant was very nicely decorated in an old world theme

Out of the Darkness

and Callie loved it. Their small corner table was nestled between pots of greenery and gave the impression of seclusion. The food was excellent and lived up to its advertisement.

When they finished their meal, to Callie's surprise, Marc suggested they take a walk down Main Street and look at the store windows all lit up with their Christmas decorations.

"Do you think you can walk in those heels?"

"Sure, but if I had known you were going to be so adventurous, I would have worn my running shoes," she teased.

"I'm glad you didn't know," he laughed. "You look very pretty. I don't think running shoes would've complimented this lovely dress," he commented as he pulled her arm through his.

Arm in arm, they took their time, stopping to look into each window. The trees and Christmas scenes were a delight to Callie and she expressed her pleasure.

"Thank you, Marc, for bringing me here. The food was delicious and the company was the best!" she exclaimed. "And this Main Street stroll is icing on the cake."

"You are very welcome. I agree with you, by the way, especially on the company," he pulled her a little closer to his side.

Callie leaned her head against his shoulder. "What are we going to do Marc? We're both loving our time together but you still live in Ohio and I live here. What are we going to do about it?" she repeated.

"It'll work out. Don't worry about it. Let's not ruin a perfect night by thinking on the what if's," he commented.

"I won't," she agreed, but couldn't help thinking of Marc's departure.

They continued their trek down the street until the occasional drifting snowflake became a steady onslaught of tiny biting pieces of icy snow. Before it got worse, Marc decided it might be best if they headed for the farm.

By the time they left town, the sidewalk and roadway were covered and the tire tracks were visible in the new snow.

When they pulled into the driveway at the farm, the snow had deepened considerably. With the lights still on in most of the house Callie knew her dad was waiting up for her.

Before they left the car, Callie turned to her date, "Do you want to come in for coffee?"

"No, thanks. This is a real date. I'm taking you to your door, telling you goodnight, and then going to my home in the barn."

She smiled at his statement and allowed him to help her from the car. The snow had deepened but Callie was still able to navigate without slipping.

"Thank you, Callie, for a wonderful evening. This won't be our last, I promise."

Callie tiptoed and kissed his shaven cheek that smelled very nice with his cologne. "And, I thank you," she whispered and slipped inside the house.

Her dad called from the living room. "Come in here, Daughter, and tell me all about your date."

Callie went straight to the living room, still wearing her cape.

"I'm glad you're home. The snow is picking up. We're supposed to get about a foot of the white stuff tonight," her dad informed her.

"You're right, Dad. It's getting mean out there."

"Sit down, Callie. Tell me about your evening," he invited.

"We went to a steakhouse in Jackson. It was a very nice night."

"Jackson! Why that's seventy miles from here," he declared.

"Yep. We had a wonderful time. After we ate, we walked down Main Street and window shopped. The stores were all closed but the windows were decorated and all lit up. It was so pretty."

"You're happy, aren't you," he commented rather than asked.

"I am, Dad. Marc is a wonderful man. He is so kind but he's strong at the same time."

Out of the Darkness

"I agree. I think he is exactly the person you need in your life. I believe he can make you happy," he predicted.

"But, Dad, I wasn't unhappy before Marc came here," she remarked.

"No. That's not entirely true. You were contented and you made yourself satisfied. But, Callie, you needed someone of your very own."

"But, Dad, I had you," she insisted.

"Yes, you did. But, Daughter, that's not the same as having a mate. Believe me, I know. No one will ever take the place of my Tess. But you're young, pretty, and healthy. You need a husband, your own home, your own kitchen."

"Dad, are you tired of me being here? Are you throwing me out?" she asked, bewildered.

"Of course not! I'd like nothing better than for you and Marc to marry and move in here with me. But that's not usually the way things work out, Honey. We live in Michigan but the man you love lives in Ohio. You have some decisions to make."

"I may not have to worry about it, Dad. Marc hasn't asked me for a commitment like that."

"That's just a formality. It's just a matter of time," he advised.

Callie went to bed with a mind full of questions. Questions not caused by Marc but by her dad. Was he tired of her taking care of him? Always being there to take up the slack that would have been her mother's job? Was he trying to get rid of her or was he trying to prepare her if and when Marc proposed marriage? Which case scenario, she couldn't decide, but was keenly aware that her perfect date with Marc had been erased by the truths presented by her dad.

Chapter 20

On Sunday morning, Callie's sleepy little town had awakened to more than a foot of beautiful snow. She loved it but fretted about the possibility of missing church.

She cooked breakfast and sent Marc a text telling him breakfast was ready. Within minutes, he joined them and just as they sat down to eat, all three of their cell phones rang.

Their pastor called and sent out a plea to every male member of the church to join together and dig out the town. It wasn't a church service but it was still helping out the town, especially the widows and the nursing home that was filled with aging residents.

The two men ate their breakfast quickly, then started piling on clothes for warmth, so they could answer the call to help their neighbors.

Her dad left to warm up the tractor, leaving Callie and Marc alone.

"How did you sleep last night, Callie?"

"So, so. Dad and I had a talk when I got home. He has such a way of making me face reality," she confided.

"He only has your best interest in mind, I'm sure."

"I know."

"I was hoping we could go to church together this morning, but the weather changed all that," he smiled.

"Yes, and you know who controls the weather," she reminded him.

"Yes, ma'am, I sure do. I guess I better go catch up to your dad. I hear his tractor."

Out of the Darkness

"Wait!" Callie reached into the cabinet and took down a thermos. She filled it to the top with hot coffee."

"Thank you. You are always taking care of us. I think it's about time we took care of you." He took the thermos, kissed her cheek, and left her to spend the morning alone.

While they were gone, Callie cleared the table and prepared a large pan of potato soup. She knew they would be cold and hungry when they returned. She turned on the radio and listened to two sermons and several hymns. It was not her usual Sunday worship, but it was better than nothing.

It was more than four hours later before she heard the tractor in the driveway and make its way on to the barn. When the men came into the house, Callie met them with large mugs of hot coffee.

"Here, drink this so you can thaw out. When you're warmed up, we can eat."

They soon sat at the table and Callie was quietly amused at their appetite. They always ate heartily but today they tackled their food like they were afraid it would get away. She remembered in her teenage years when she would help shovel their driveway after a heavy snow and how famished she would be afterward. She knew snow shoveling was hard work, no matter the age.

As Callie was clearing the table with Marc's help, her dad made a suggestion.

"Since we missed our worship this morning, I'm going to have my devotions. Do you kids want to join me?"

Without needing to think about it, Callie and Marc agreed at the same time. Callie put the dishes in the sink to be finished later. She knew Marc's Bible was in his room, so she picked up her mother's Bible from a table in the living room and handed it to him.

They sat around the kitchen table and waited for her dad to settle on a passage. Callie was thrilled when he chose Second Corinthians chapter twelve and verse nine. He read the entire verse, then went back to the first line, *My grace is sufficient for thee.* He spoke of many instances in his

165

life how God's Word had proven to be enough. His voice quivered as he recounted God's grace when Dirk died, but he couldn't hold back the tears when he spoke of the death of his beloved Tessa.

Callie reached for a table napkin and dried her own eyes. When Marc sniffed across the table, she slid him a napkin, too. Her dad had never tried to hide his grief, but he, also, had never failed to give God praise for seeing him through it.

"After all we've been through, we're still standing, aren't we!" He directed his comment to the young couple seated at the table.

"I'm still standing," Callie smiled and looked at Marc.

He reached across the table and took her hand.

"Yes, I'm still standing. I thought I'd never get to where I am now. You both have helped me more than you'll ever know. The more I watched and listened, I realized how empty I was. Then the day came when I realized my real need was Christ alone. My world and outlook was forever changed," he finished quietly.

Callie squeezed his hand in response and he returned the pressure. Her heart nearly burst at his words. It was the first time that she'd heard him really talk about his salvation and she wouldn't have missed it for the world.

Though the snow storm was over and some of the roads had been made passable, the frigid temperature kept everyone closed in. Callie knew what her dad would do. He'd turn on a ball game, kick back in his recliner, and promptly fall asleep. He didn't disappoint her. Marc, she wasn't so sure about. Would he go to his room in the barn, or would he stay in the house? She was very pleased when he suggested they play a numbers game that she hadn't played in years.

"Oh, I love that game! We used to play it when Dirk was alive. After he died, Mom and I would play it some, then....well, you know. My dad couldn't bring himself to play it anymore. I didn't badger him about it. So, we put the game away."

"Will it bother you too much, Callie?" he asked. "I saw the game on a shelf in your Mom's little sitting room, I just thought...."

Out of the Darkness

"No! I love to play that game, but Dad doesn't care for board games. Well, he did at one time, but not anymore."

"Are you any good at it?" he teased.

"I used to be," she admitted, "but it's been a long time."

"Uh-huh, I bet," he teased more.

"No, really," Callie refuted. "I haven't played in years."

"Well, we'll check out your expertise," he laughed.

For the next three hours, they played. Sometimes there was laughter, at times serious concentration, but mostly, they talked. With every conversation that occurred, Callie found out more about him. This time, she found out he had a fierce competitiveness that she suspected helped him as an attorney. The only difference was when she won a game, he was still sweet to her. She doubted he teased and flirted with someone who had just bested him in the court room. She chuckled at the thought.

The frigid weather stuck around for days preventing the snow from melting, but the roads were getting more clear daily from the wear of the big truck tires and the road graders.

On Tuesday, Callie was positive that she could take her dad's truck and make the two mile trek to her shop in town, but Marc would have no part of it. He took her to work, not just on Tuesday but everyday that week. She didn't need him to take her but she surely did enjoy it.

There were more snows which Callie was used to. Even a skiff of snow and Marc was waiting, with his vehicle warmed up, to drive her to work. She knew it was just an excuse to be with her and she took full advantage of it.

Callie had grown so used to him being around that she nearly forgot that it would end when the new year began. Little did she suspect that it would end sooner.

One week before Christmas, Callie was already full of the Christmas spirit. Their home was decorated, not only, with the large tree in the living room but a small tree was in every window. Marc had helped her wrap the columns on the front porch with colored lights, and the front shrubs were covered with netted lights. Callie was enjoying Christmas more than any since her mother had been gone. The only change was Marc. He made her want to live life to the fullest, and she was a willing participant.

On Thursday afternoon when Marc showed up at her salon looking worried and strained, she knew instantly something was wrong.

"Callie, my Mom called. My Dad has had a heart attack and is in the hospital," he rushed his words.

"Oh, no, Marc! I am so sorry. How bad is he?"

"I'm not sure. It only happened a couple hours ago and they're still running tests," he informed her. "Honey, I have to go."

"Of course, you do," she agreed. "You need to hurry and pack your things."

"I've already done that. Callie, I don't want to leave you, but Mom needs me," he hedged.

"Of course you do. Your place is with her," she replied, trying hard not to let him see the pain she was feeling as she was blindsided by truth and reality.

"I don't guess you'd want to come with me?" he asked.

"Marc, I can't," she whispered. Then found her voice. "Your Mom and Dad need you, so you need to go to them. My dad needs me, so I stay here. Deep down, Marc, we both knew it would end this way."

"Callie, it's not ending. I just have to go see about them and do what I can to help them. I'll be back," he insisted.

"No, Marc. You won't be back. Your home is in Ohio and mine is in rural Michigan. I'll never forget you, Marc, but you need to go," she prompted.

"But, Callie...I want to have a future with you. I want to have a family with you, this is not the end," he insisted.

"That can't happen, Marc. Our families need us and that's the way it has to be," she concluded.

"Callie, don't..." he started.

Out of the Darkness

"You've got to go, Marc. I will be praying for your dad. Please drive carefully," she dismissed him.

He stared at her, then turned and left the shop.

Callie was so glad there were no customers to witness the exchange between her and Marc. Her next customer was due any minute. She didn't have a chance to give in to the pain she was experiencing, but she knew as soon as her last customer left the shop, a good cry was coming.

Chapter 21

Three days later, Callie's dad questioned her. "You miss him, don't you?"

"Yes," she admitted.

"Why don't you call him? I know he's been calling constantly, but you won't answer. Why don't you call him?" he repeated.

"No. It's better to have a clean break. The last thing he needs is a weepy female hanging on to something that can't happen."

"Well, Callie. I'm going to be up front with you. I have talked to Marc. Everyday as a matter of fact. His dad had a serious heart attack. They put in two stents, kept him over night, and sent him home. He's going to have to slow down. Maybe not work so much. Start a walking regimen, and watch his diet. You know the drill."

"I'm so sorry for Mr. Grant. He's an extra nice man."

"He is, and so is his son," he watched her reaction.

"I know he is, Dad."

"Well, why don't you call him and talk to him? He misses you."

"Dad, Marc is not coming back. You might as well accept it," she adamantly stated. Her dad didn't comment on her outburst, but surprised her with his next statement.

"I'm thinking about going to see them. I've become good friends with the Grants and I think I might take me a little trip."

"Dad!" she exclaimed. "Why would you do that when I'm trying to get over Marc? You know it's going to hurt my feelings if you go. Besides, it's three days until Christmas. That's not a good time to visit anyone."

Out of the Darkness

"Callie, this is not all about you. They're my friends, too. You don't have to go. I'm not even going to ask that of you. But, I'm going. I've already talked to John and Ed. They're going to take turns checking on the cows. They're going to feed Wally and check on Lizzie and try to keep her boy inside the fence."

"Dad, I can't believe we're having this conversation. You've always been fair and kind to me, but now, you're choosing strangers over your own daughter," she began to cry.

He watched her cry, not offering an apology at her tears. When he made no move to comfort her, she became embarrassed and hurried from the room.

In her room, she experienced so many emotions that she probably couldn't have named them all. She was angry. She was hurt. Embarrassment was mixed with frustration. She felt all of these but mostly she felt loneliness. She missed Marc. She needed him, but what could she do about it? He was there attending to his responsibilities and she was here doing the same. She prayed. Pouring her heart out to the Lord, she asked for answers and guidance.

She was too embarrassed to leave her bedroom for the remainder of the night. She was ashamed of her outburst with her Dad. Sleep didn't come easy. She could close her eyes, but that couldn't stop her mind from replaying the hateful words spoken to the man who had been both mom and dad to her. No matter what happened with Marc, this disagreement she had caused with her dad had to be repaired. Even if she never saw or heard from Marc again, she had to apologize to her dad. She had been taught the Ten Commandments as a child, and honoring her father was very important. She knew exactly what she had to do.

****

Callie was up early, even before daybreak. She had barely slept, but sleep was the farthest thing from her mind. She busied herself cooking her dad's favorite breakfast, as a way to add to her apology that was coming.

When her dad came in to the kitchen, Callie was waiting.

"Dad, may I talk to you?" she asked nervously.

"Sure, if that's what you want to do."

"I'm sorry, Dad, for last night. I acted like a spoiled brat. I shouldn't have said those things to you. I was unfair. I was frustrated and I took it out on you. I need your forgiveness."

"Callie, I knew you didn't mean those words, even as you were saying them," he comforted her. "But, Honey, you sent Marc away. So what is causing all this frustration and hurt?"

"It's him. It's Marc," her face crumpled in tears. "I miss him!"

"Callie, be honest with me. Most importantly, be honest with yourself. Do you love him?" he probed.

"Yes!" she wept openly. "I love him but his home is in Ohio and mine is here."

"Are you trying to tell me that you love him but you won't go with him wherever his work takes him?" he asked bluntly.

"That's right. I can't leave here."

"Why not?" he quipped.

"Dad? You can ask me that? I can't leave my childhood home, my business, this town, but mostly, Dad, I can't leave you."

"Are you kidding me?" he barked. "Callie, if you love Marc and he loves you, your place is to be with him. Nothing else is as important as that."

"But, Dad, I can't leave you alone," she teared up again.

"And why not? Daughter, I'm not a little boy. I can take care of myself," he stressed. He paused for the longest time, making Callie wonder what he was going to say next.

"Callie, I've done you an injustice. This is all my fault." At her confused look, he continued. "Honey, when your mama died, it was so easy to let you take care of everything. You did it so well. You took care of me, the house, the meals and everything. You kept the house running without a flaw. I was grateful to let you do it. But, Callie, it's time for me to man up and take over. There's that little cleaning service that started up in town.

I can get them to come and clean every week or two. Depends on how messy I am," he chuckled. "And, I know the way to Hannah's," he smiled.

"Do you mean that you don't care if I move to be with Marc?" she ventured to ask.

"Callie, I'd miss you if you moved next door, but that's beside the point. If you love each other, then you belong together."

"Dad, I have a question. May I go with you to Ohio?" she grinned.

"When do you want to leave?" He grinned right back at her.

"Today is Thursday, I can move my Friday's appointments to today. I can go tomorrow, if you can wait."

"I can wait," he hugged her.

Callie grinned. "Today will be busy. I was thinking of closing tomorrow anyway. I can be ready tomorrow. It will be the day before Christmas Eve. Let's surprise them," she suggested.

"Okay," he agreed.

With a lighter heart and burden, Callie hurried with the breakfast dishes and left early for work. She had several calls to make to change appointments. When all appointments had been changed, she squared her shoulders and prepared for a long busy day. Looking forward to the trip ahead of her, Callie was able to join in on all the Christmas festivities that her clients brought with them into the salon. As her stack of baked goods and sweets grew, she knew she'd not need to bake any sweets for the holidays. Her customers were bringing in so much food, she knew most of it would need to go in the freezer.

It was way past dark when Callie closed the door behind her last customer. She unplugged the Christmas tree but left one light shining on the manger scene that was in the window. She gathered the wet towels and bagged them to take home with her. She usually washed and dried them at the shop but not this time. She was in a hurry to get home and pack for her trip.

The baked goods and gifts were boxed up and carried to her car. On her final trip to the car, she paused at the door and looked around. This shop had been her dream and she loved working here. It could soon be coming to an end and she would miss it, but not as much as she missed Marc. She locked the door without shedding a sentimental tear.

At home, her dad helped her carry in her load of food and gifts. Callie went directly to the laundry room and tossed her towels in the washer. She went straight back to the kitchen and stopped short.

"Dad! I forgot to stop and get our dinner from Hannah's!"

"I knew you were going to have a long day, so I made a call to Hannah myself. I ordered us some dinner and it's waiting in the oven," he announced proudly.

"Oh, Dad, you're a life saver," she laughed.

"See? I told you I could take care of myself! And I can take care of my little girl," he smiled.

"No doubt about that," she reached and squeezed his hand.

They ate and made plans at the same time. Callie had a pen and pad and made a list of things they wanted to take with them.

"Dad, how long do you think we'll be staying?"

"I thought we'd come home the day after Christmas. What do you think about that time line?" he tossed the question back to her.

"I think that should be enough time to see...Dad, what if he doesn't want me anymore? I mean...I did send him away," she worried.

"I'd say, yes, he still wants you, but we'll go see what happens." He paused. "Honey, I probably shouldn't tell you this but he's called everyday to check on you."

"Really?" she asked, bewildered.

"Yes, but I wish you wouldn't let him know I told you. He didn't say not to tell you but I think it was meant to be just man to man."

"Of course," she nodded.

Callie went to her room and laid out what she wanted to take with her. Next, she went to her dad's room and found him in his closet and his suitcase open on the floor.

"Dad, do you need some help?"

"No. No, I got it. Your mama took care of me, then you took me on when she had to leave. I think I need to start taking care of myself," he announced proudly.

"Oh, Dad," she whispered.

"Go on," he urged. "Pack for yourself. Callie, I think we need to take those gifts under our Christmas tree with us, just in case they let us spend Christmas with them. What do you think?"

"I'd love that," Callie agreed.

Callie went to bed, too excited to sleep. She thought of Marc and how good it was going to be to see him. Had it only been a week? It seemed like months since she'd told him it was pretty well over.

The alarm sounded and Callie sat straight up in her bed. She looked at her clock and couldn't believe she'd slept the night through. The blankets seemed heavy and she turned them back and stood up.

Fully awake now, Callie's mind went to the trip scheduled for later in the day. The thought of seeing Marc thrilled her but scared her at the same time. What would be her reception when they got to Ohio? She had no idea, but she knew she was supposed to make the trip.

Callie made her bed and headed for the kitchen. To her surprise, her dad was seated at the table with a coffee cup in front of him.

"Dad! How long have you been up?"

"About thirty minutes or so. You want a cup of coffee?" he offered.

"You made coffee?"

"Don't look so surprised! I can make coffee."

"But...you've never made it before," she sputtered.

"I know. I've never had to before. I think it's time I started doing more for myself," he declared.

"Oh, Dad. I love making your morning coffee."

Debrah Gish

"I know, Daughter, I know. Marc taught me how to make coffee. The first pot was a disaster," he chuckled. "I spilled coffee all over the counter. Marc helped me clean it up so you wouldn't know about it," he laughed even harder. "The second try was a success."

"Dad! I can't believe you two have been keeping secrets from me," she scolded playfully.

"Only just some little ones," he admitted.

"Well, Dad, would you allow me to cook you some breakfast?" she teased.

"Sure. Be my guest. While you cook, I'll find a place in my truck for all those Christmas gifts." He got up and put on his coat.

"Dad, don't you want to go in my car? There's more back seat room," she suggested.

"I know, but we may run into some snow. If that happens, I'd rather be in my truck. Besides, taking my new truck will give me a chance to try out that fancy bed cover that I've never used," he reasoned.

Giving in, Callie quickly cooked breakfast and had it on the table when her dad finished packing the colorful packages to the truck. Within two hours, she had finished the dishes, had the house in order, and had her suitcase by the door.

As tempted as she was to check her dad's suitcase, she threw caution to the wind and left it shut. If he was determined to start taking care of himself, she would try to meet him halfway.

It was mid-morning when they finally got on their way. Callie googled the mileage to their destination and calculated the trip should take no more than five hours unless they got held up in traffic. Since they weren't being expected, they really had no schedule, but Callie knew her dad. He would be focused on their destination and would be headed for it.

Callie had not checked the weather and they did run through two snow squalls. They were brief and they weren't slowed down much at all.

As they passed through towns and eatery signs, they debated on stopping. With neither feeling hungry, they decided to wait until they

Out of the Darkness

arrived at their destination before eating. The closer they got to Columbus, Callie began to search online for hotels. She entered the hotel address into the GPS and they were led into the hotel parking lot. They drove around the parking lot without finding a parking place. Callie surmised that the hotel was full of Christmas travelers just like herself and her dad. Before leaving to find another lodging place, her dad decided to check for vacancies. He pulled in front of the brightly lit office and went inside.

He was back within ten minutes with cards in hand.

"They had one single and a suite. I took the suite," he announced.

"Dad, two vehicles have left the parking lot. If we hurry, we may be able to find one of the empty spots," she instructed. He followed where Callie pointed and parked.

"Let's go in and get settled before we eat, then we'll try to find the Grants. How does that sound?"

"Sounds good, Dad. I just hope...," she trailed off.

"Don't worry about a thing. God is in control, Callie, you know that."

"I know. Well, let's go inside, I'm getting hungry," she laughed.

They got settled into their suite and Callie took the time to hang up some of her clothes and hung up her dad's clothes without him even noticing.

They found an Italian restaurant that belonged to a well known chain and decided to eat there. The food was good but they both agreed that this eatery didn't have anything on their Hannah back home.

Even though Callie was nervous, she had to admit it was nice to be out and in a large city at Christmas time. The decorations were everywhere and they were beautiful.

Not knowing the town, Callie put the Grant's address into the GPS and let the lady lead the way. They made several turns and it was apparent they had entered an affluent part of the town. Large beautiful homes with spacious lawns lined the street. The lawns were so large that the houses were not close together.

The GPS lady directed them into the driveway of a large white two story house with huge columns. They pulled into the driveway and parked. Callie looked at her dad.

"Do you think this is it, Dad?"

"Only one way to find out. Are you going with me, Honey?" he looked at her.

"I am. If this is the wrong house, I'm not going to let you be the only one embarrassed," she smiled.

They climbed from the truck and walked side by side up to the tall front door. Her dad rang the doorbell and only then did Callie feel the massive group of butterflies that attacked her stomach.

Chapter 22

Callie and her dad waited before the tall double doors and were beginning to think, either no one was home or else they didn't want company. They turned to leave just as the door opened behind them.

Mrs. Grant stared at them as if she couldn't believe what she was seeing. "Callie! Tom! What...How...What in the world brings you here?" she finally managed to say.

"Well, we wanted to come and check on Dan and to wish you all a Merry Christmas," Tom Hinson responded.

"Oh, please, forgive me. Won't you please, please come in. My it is so good to see both of you! Dan is going to be so pleased to see you." She led the way into a large foyer that held a grandfather clock on one side and and a slim ornate table on the other. The foyer opened into a room filled with comfy overstuffed chairs and sofas.

"Dan, look who's here! They came all this way to check on you. Isn't it wonderful?" she announced to her husband who was dressed in pajamas and a robe and was resting on a sofa with fluffy pillows behind him.

Mrs. Grant caught Callie looking around the room.

"I know who you're looking for. He's in his room. Follow me, Honey." She led Callie into a spacious snow-white kitchen with large windows beside the breakfast nook.

"Sit here, Callie. I'll send him in. I don't think you two need an audience when you see each other after being apart," Marc's mother commented thoughtfully and left the room.

Callie waited and almost immediately, Marc came through another door. He stopped short and for the first time since she had met him, he seemed uncertain of himself.

Callie stood and went to him. "Hello, Marc."

"Callie, what are you doing here?" he managed to say.

"I...we wanted to come and see about your Dad, and," she paused, "we'd like to spend Christmas with you, if we would be allowed to."

"You know the answer to that," he reached for her and she willingly stepped closer to him.

"Marc, can we talk? I have so much to say."

"I have a lot to say, too, Callie," he assured her.

"Me first, okay? Let's sit here at the table and I want to tell you something. Please," she implored.

They sat across from each other at the small table. Callie reached her hands across the table and Marc clasped them.

"Marc, I am so sorry I said those things to you last week. I was so wrong. I've told myself since my Mom died that I could never leave my dad. But I had never been in love before. When I sent you away alone, I realized that my place is with you. If your work is here in Ohio, or somewhere else, I'll close my shop and follow you wherever you go. I can talk to my dad everyday if I want to and we can visit him. But, I want to be with you," she paused. "Well, that's what I came to say," she finished.

"So, you love me?" he asked with his eyes twinkling.

"Yes, I do."

"How do you know it's not the same thing you felt for poor old Kent Phillips," he asked, half teasing but serious at the same time.

"Because when Kent left, I didn't give it another thought. When you left I cried for three days until dad convinced me to come and see you and tell you what's in my heart," she admitted.

"Oh, Honey, I appreciate everything you just said. It's wonderful to know that I'm first in your life. But the truth is, you're not going to have to make those decisions," he stated.

Callie's eyes widened. "I'm sorry. I thought you and I, we....," she stood to leave.

"Wait! Hold on! The reason you're not going to have to choose is because I'm coming back to your town. I'm moving there permanently. A few weeks ago I went and talked to your town attorney, Mr. Thomas, to see if he thought there could be enough business for a second lawyer in your town. He told me he wanted to retire but couldn't because the town would be without an attorney. He offered to sell me his practice and I jumped at the chance. So I'll be living and practicing law in your town," he happily informed her.

"Does my dad know this?" she asked bewildered.

"No. I had to tell my dad first because in actuality, he is my boss. Other than my parents, I haven't told anyone. I wanted to tell you first."

"But, Marc, what about your parents? They don't have anyone but you. You can't leave them," she countered.

"Well," he laughed, "you're not going to believe this, but my Dad is selling his law firm to his partners. They're also selling this house and moving with me."

"Really? That's hard to believe, Marc," she exclaimed.

"No, Callie, it's the truth. They don't want to live away from me. They fell in love with your town and everything about it. Just like I fell in love with you," his voice lowered to a whisper.

"So, you love me?" She repeated to him what he had asked her.

"You better believe I do," he grinned.

"I'm so glad to be here," she admitted. "I am sorry we didn't let you know we were coming. We should've called first."

"Why? You and your dad are more than welcome here anytime."

"I was hoping we would be. We...well, I wanted to spend Christmas with you, and you couldn't leave your mom alone with your dad still recovering. So here we are," she grinned sheepishly.

"I am so glad to see you. I'll help your dad bring in your luggage."

"No," Callie interrupted. "We've checked into a hotel a few blocks away."

"No! You didn't!" he declared.

"Yes. We really did. Your Mom and you have been through a lot with your dad's heart attack. We thought it would be too much. So we checked into a hotel," she explained.

"Still, we would rather you were staying here."

Callie reached for his hands again. "I can't believe I'm here with you," she grinned.

"I was thinking the same thing. I'm so glad you came," he said softly.

"Me, too."

"Callie, you'll never know what you've done for me. You saved my life," he said bluntly. At her confused look, he held her hands and continued. "When I showed up in your woods, I had no idea what I was going to do or what was going to happen to me. I felt hopeless and was helpless to do anything about it. You didn't know you were doing anything but you were slowly leading me out of the darkness. Then you led me to the One that could finish fixing me. I can't believe my life now. I'm happy. I'm a Christian. I have peace and contentment that I am so thankful for. And I'm in love with the sweetest, kindest, most beautiful woman that God ever created." He raised her hands to his lips.

"Oh, Marc, I think I'm going to cry," she whispered.

"Well, don't do that!" he teased. "What about you? Are you happy?"

"My goodness, yes!" she laughed. "I was happy, I thought, when you came to our woods. I was content and had the joy of the Lord, but I admit, I didn't really know what happiness was. Now I do," she admitted.

They sat quietly, each one having their own thoughts.

Out of the Darkness

"Let's go see the folks," he commented. Marc stood and held out his hand.

Callie agreed and gave him her hand, along with her heart.

****

Callie and her dad spent nearly every waking moment at the Grants. Their visit couldn't have gone better. When they had arrived, there were no Christmas decorations to be seen. At Laura Grant's suggestion, their boxed Christmas tree was dragged from an upstairs closet and set up in front of the floor to ceiling windows that faced the street. Callie helped Marc and his mother decorate the tree while the two dads coached from the sidelines. She had brought the baked goods and sweets given to her by her customers and they were now on display on the counter of the pristine white kitchen of the Grant home. The gifts that had been hauled with them from Michigan now rested beneath the newly decorated tree.

Early on Christmas Eve, Marc, Callie, and Mrs. Grant went shopping downtown while Tom Hinson played nursemaid to his ailing friend.

Mrs. Grant separated from her shopping mates, but Marc and Callie stayed together while he shopped for his mom and dad, along with Callie's dad. At the appointed time, the couple met up with the older woman and helped her carry her two bulging bags.

At home, Mrs. Grant holed up in her bedroom to wrap her gifts, while Marc and Callie took over the kitchen to wrap his purchases.

In the afternoon, Marc made a request of Callie. "Next year on Christmas Eve, I want you to make me some of your delicious chili. Will you?"

"I certainly will!" she promised. Then she had an idea, "You can have chili this Christmas Eve if you'll take me to the supermarket."

"Don't tempt me," he laughed.

"I'm not kidding. If you want chili, I'll make it."

"Sweetheart, you're on. Get your coat."

Callie had never been in such a large supermarket. The deli alone was as big as the entire supermarket at home. She was in her element as she chose the ingredients for their dinner. They decided to buy for their Christmas dinner, as well, so the two women would not spend their day cooking. They chose turkey and chicken from the deli and an assortment of salads to accommodate Mr. Grant's newly prescribed diet.

They returned to the house and Marc helped Callie chop, saute, and mix together the ingredients for her chili. While it simmered, they had time to enjoy coffee and some of Callie's shared pastries.

The chili was delicious and only Marc and Callie knew that the dish was made with health conscience ingredients because of Mr. Grant's condition.

The five sat around the Christmas tree and enjoyed quiet conversation until bedtime. Callie and her dad went back to their hotel with the promise to be back for breakfast on Christmas morning.

To Callie's joy, they woke up to a snow covered Christmas. She knew her dad's truck would have no trouble traveling on the light snow, so she didn't try to hide her excitement of having a white Christmas.

They arrived back at the Grants as promised and were met by a fretting Marc. "I was worried you wouldn't be able to make it," he confessed.

"You forget that I grew up in rural Michigan. On days like this, we don't even cancel school," she laughed.

They had coffee and pastries in the kitchen to stave off the hungers until brunch which would be after gift opening time.

They gathered around the lighted tree in the spacious family room and Marc was chosen to pass out the gifts. Mrs. Grant was visibly touched by the gifts given to her by Callie. She stood immediately and put on the soft pink cashmere sweater. She admired the leather covered Bible with her name imprinted on the front, and touched it reverently.

Callie was equally surprised at the purse given to her by Marc's parents. A tasteful white bathrobe was also opened and a box of her favorite chocolates was added to her growing pile of gifts.

The Bible Callie gave to Marc was passed around and made its way back to its owner and he openly admired it. His second gift was a light blue dress shirt with his initials monogrammed on the pocket and matching tie. Callie leaned over to him.

"That looks like a lawyer's shirt," she said softly.

"Do you know one?" he teased.

"Oh, I do! I really like him, too," she whispered.

Their parents were carrying on their own conversation while Marc and Callie talked between themselves.

"Callie, let's go to the kitchen for a minute." Marc reached for her hand she followed him to the adjoining room. He closed the door behind them, then turned to her.

"I wanted to be alone with you for a reason. This is so private and so important to me that I didn't want anyone listening. We've not had a conventional relationship. We didn't really date. Well, not very much anyway. But I do know that I love you more than anyone else in this world. I think about you when I'm not with you. From morning until night, I'm thinking about a life with you. You're everything to me. You brought me to know Christ and then Christ gave me this love I have for you. I can't see a future without you in it. I love you and I want to marry you. Would you even consider being married to a young lawyer just striking out on his own?" he finished.

"Marc, I love you, too. Yes, I would consider being married to a tenderfoot lawyer, as long as it was you. Nothing would make me happier than being Mrs. Marc Grant." She tried to hold back her tender emotions but failed.

Marc used his thumbs to wipe the errant tears that slipped from her eyes. He stepped away from her and opened a cupboard door briefly. Returning to her with a small white velvet box, he opened the tiny lid and lifted the diamond ring from its nest.

"Will you marry me, Callie?" he whispered.

"Yes," she whispered her answer.

Debrah Gish

He slipped the ring on her finger and held her close. For the first time since they met, he kissed her. The kiss was full of love and promise. Callie knew this man that she loved, this man who had not so long ago lived in a very dark place, had been led from that place by the only One that could. Now the same God that rescued Marc had brought them together with a love that could only come from their Heavenly Father.

Epilogue

Two Years Later...

The farm house was bustling with laughter and the happiness within those walls was so thick, it could nearly be felt.

Callie divided her time between the group gathered in the living room and checking on her Christmas dinner cooking in the kitchen. Marc was a huge help to her and lifted all the heavy pans. He helped her spread the tablecloth and set the table in the dining room with her mother's Christmas china.

"Are you ready for me to go get my mom? You know she wants to help," he insisted.

"No, Honey. I'm okay. I really am. Besides you're helping me." She leaned toward him and kissed him briefly on the lips. "She's really enjoying herself. Let her continue holding the baby."

"Those three adults in there are watching that little pink blanket like they're afraid she'll disappear. If she wiggles or grunts, they all jump and run," Marc laughed.

"I know," Callie joined his laughter. "That little girl is only six weeks old, but she's the boss of those three grown ups in the next room."

"I must admit, she's the boss of her daddy, too. I guess you're going to have to be the boss of our little princess," he admitted.

Callie slipped her arms around him and hugged him.

"You are such a good daddy. She's one blessed little girl," Callie smiled.

"You know, Honey, two years ago when you agreed to marry me, I thought I could never be happier, but I was wrong. Being married to you for nearly two years has been more wonderful than I ever dreamed. Then six weeks ago, you gave me this little pink bundle. I thought my heart couldn't contain all that love," he declared.

"I know I feel the same way. God has been so good to us. Your law practice is going great. Your mom and dad built their new house just down the road. More importantly, they both have become Christians. You had a talk with my dad about our future...and his. So, here we are, all living together in my childhood home. But, remember, Marc, if you ever want to move elsewhere, I'll start packing," she reminded him.

"I remember, but I can't see us ever moving out. You love it here, I love it here, so why move. Your dad loves having us here and he needs us. Even though he would deny it," he laughed.

"That's true. And, don't forget, Jamey will grow up here. She'll watch the cows and learn the farm life, just like I did. I think farm life is good for children."

"Our own baby! Can you believe it, Callie? We are a family. You've made all this possible. You even named our little girl after my brother. He would be so honored. Mom and dad can't get over your generosity with the baby. You allow them to visit anytime. Actually, you encourage it."

"Oh, well," she dismissed. "I have been so blessed, that I can't help but share it. Sometime, I feel like I must be dreaming. But I reach out and touch you and you're real. I feel my little girl in my arms, and I know she's real. As far as the name, I think it suits her. I never met him, but he will always be around through his namesake. She will always be a reminder of the brother that you love. Besides, she's a Grant through and through. I may have carried her and birthed her but she's her daddy's girl. All the way from the head full of black hair, to her gorgeous eyes to her stubborn personality," she teased.

He looked down at her. "For some reason, I don't think you're complaining," he bragged.

"No," she laughed. "I'm not complaining."

"I love you," he whispered.

"I know it," she whispered back," and I love you, too."

"Dinner is ready. Do you think we can pry those three away from their granddaughter?" Callie asked.

Out of the Darkness

"I seriously doubt it. I'm betting her infant carrier will be occupying that sixth chair at the table," he predicted.

"And that's how it should be. We both have some missing family members, but God has given us more family. He's growing our family with love and that's the only kind to have," she spoke from the heart.

Together they went to the living room to see which grandparent was in possession of their daughter.

Callie knew only God could bring complete strangers together and love would spring up between them. She and Marc were living that kind of life, blessed by the One that could turn hate to love, change bad to good, and bring a person out of darkness into His light.

Other Books by Debrah Gish
- *All of Our Tomorrows – ISBN: 978-1643490441*
- *In the Potter's Hands – ISBN: 978-1098001148*
- *Amelia's Prayer – ISBN: 978-1098066772*
- *Love's Healing Power – ISBN: 979-8889435648*

Printed in the USA
CPSIA information can be obtained
at www.ICGtesting.com
LVHW090028201024
794167LV00002B/230